Dear, Vanity 2:

Echon's Return

D1539293

Nona Day

SOUL Publications

SOUL Publications

1 Year Later

Vanity

"EJ, have you got everything packed," I yelled at him from the kitchen.

He was going to spend his Spring break with Tree. This would be the first time he's gone away for an entire week. I know he would be in good hands, but I was sad and nervous about him being away from me for so long. Yes, I was definitely a overprotective mother. Every day I look at him I see so much of his father in him. I didn't cry anymore when I thought of Echon. Only happiness filled my heart remembering the love we shared. My only regret is that our time with each other was so limited. I was so blessed to be left with a blessing as a reminder of what we shared.

"Stop running in the house!" I yelled when I heard him running down the hallway. He was super excited about going to New Orleans for his vacation. He walked into the kitchen dragging his suitcase.

"Mama, I could've packed my things," he said sitting at the kitchen table. I stayed up late last night making sure he had everything he needed for his trip.

SOUL Publications

"Yea, and we would've been late this morning," I said sitting his plate of breakfast in front of him. He laughed because he knew I was telling the truth.

"Mama, my bacon isn't done," he said looking at his food. That was another thing he inherited from his father. He liked all his meat almost burnt.

I snickered and shook my head. I took the bacon off the plate and wrapped it in napkins before sticking it in the microwave. After sitting back down with him at the table, we talked about school and sports. I was thankful for Quran being a great role model in his life when it came to sports. I attended all of his games, but Quran was the one that made sure he was at every practice. Quran is a great man, but he wasn't the man for me. I could never disrespect Echon by having a romantic relationship with his friend. He finally gave up his quest of taking me on a date. I was grateful it didn't damage our friendship and business relationship.

"What's the golden rule?" I asked him as he ate.

He looked up at me giving me his father's smile. "Be kind and always show respect and appreciation." I nodded my head.

Dear, Vanity 2: Echon's Return   Nona Day

"Uncle Tree called me last night. We talked about all the fun stuff we are going to do while I'm there. I wish you could come with us," he said.

"Me too, but I have to work. We'll visit together in the summer," I said winking at him.

"Uncle Q said you don't have to work if you don't want to. He said Daddy left you with a lot of money," he said. That infuriated me. I made a mental note to speak to Quran about the things he shares with EJ about Echon.

"Your father left the money to make sure we have everything we need. It's not so we can be lazy. I want you to know that hard work builds great character," I said.

"I'm going to work hard to be a pro football or basketball player," he said smiling.

Whichever one you chose I know you'll be the best. I'm going to be your biggest cheerleader," I said. He laughed and blushed.

"I feel bad leaving you here alone," he said sadly. Just like his father, he said exactly what he felt.

"Don't feel bad. I have Tee Tee here with me. We are going to have grown folks fun while you are away."

He laughed. "Tee Tee crazy."

"Yes, she is," I said laughing with him.

When the doorbell rang, I went to answer the door. I knew it was Tree. I didn't feel comfortable putting EJ on a flight alone. I offered to fly out with him, but Tree said he would fly out to get him since he had business to handle this way. I knew what Tree did for a living, but I was no one's judge and jury. I know he would protect my son's life with his own. When I opened the door, him and Yella Boy stood there in all their swagger. They were two very handsome young men. They both gave me a hug after I invited them in. EJ came rushing toward us hauling his suitcase.

"I'm ready," he said smiling up at them. We all laughed.

"We gotta lil time to spare. No need to rush," Tree said.

"But I'm ready to see my sister," EJ said excited. He fell in love with Baby Gladys. He felt like he was her protector.

"Well, you going to have another lil sister in about six months," Tree said with a big smile on his face. My mouth dropped open with shock and excitement for him and Nika. EJ jumped up and down with joy.

Dear, Vanity 2: Echon's Return   Nona Day

"Congratulations," I said happily to him.

We all jumped when my front door came flying open. Zelda came rushing in almost out of breath. Her hair and clothes were disheveled. I knew she was coming from one of her wild and crazy nights.

"Whew Chile, I'm getting old. I barely can breathe from rushing over here," she said trying to catch her breath. I laughed. Tree and Yella Boy stood there looking at her like she was crazy. They had met Zelda before, but they didn't know here like me and EJ.

"Somebody after you?" Tree asked with concern.

"Oh no, I just had to make sure I made it here to see my lil man off," she said smiling down at EJ. She loves him like he's her own. She walked toward him to hug him.

"Don't kiss him," Yella Boy said seriously. We all gave him a confused look.

"And why the hell not?" Zelda asked with an attitude.

"By the look of you I'm pretty sure I know what you did last night. I'm almost positive you haven't brushed your teeth," he said bluntly.

Me and Tree laughed while Zelda stood there speechless. After gathering her thoughts, she cussed him out from A to Z. He stood there not being phased by anything she was saying.

"Tee Tee, I have an extra toothbrush in my bathroom you can use," EJ said. Yella Boy chuckled. She rolled her eyes at Yella Boy.

Zelda gave EJ her attention. "Thank you, Baby. Here, you use this to buy whatever you want. I'm going to miss you." She gave him a prepaid debit card and hugged him.

"He don't need money. We ain't broke," Yella Boy said.

She turned to face him. "You know what? You getting on my last nerve. That's my nephew. I give him what I want. Go lay in the damn sun and bake, nigga. Out here looking like a muscular ass banana."

Me, Tree and EJ were crying laughing as they exchanged insults. After they finished going back and forth, I gave EJ a big hug and kissed him before sending him off. I had an entire week to myself to do nothing but miss my son.

Dear, Vanity 2: Echon's Return   Nona Day

"Uh Unh, don't even think about crying. This the week you bout to get some dick," Zelda said as we stood in the parking lot watching them drive away.

Zelda

"**N**o, unplug the aux cord. We are not listening to my Granny's music while we drive to the club," I told Vanity. She laughed.

We were headed on a double date. I loved the place Vanity was in her life now. She was happy and enjoying life. I was glad she got the closure she needed to move on with her life. Not knowing Echon's fate was holding her back from living a happy life. After finding out about his death, she took it extremely hard, but she pushed through it. The only problem now is getting her to stop comparing every man that attempts to date her to Echon. I plugged up my aux cord and Lil Kim's *Lighter's Up* blasted through my speakers.

"That's old too Zelda. It's 2018," I said laughing.

"I don't care. Kim my bitch," I said bopping my head to the beat.

Vanity laughed. "I swear you think you gangsta."

"Girl, I am. I'm bout my money and some good dick like these niggas all about money and a wet pussy," I said.

Dear, Vanity 2: Echon's Return   Nona Day

To be honest I was in a place in my life where I wanted more from a man. I just have a hard time finding a man that can handle me. I don't like clingy men. I need a man that can make me drop to my knees at the feel of his masculine aura. Most men play the hardcore role until they meet a woman that doesn't give a fuck about them loving her. And I'm that bitch that's not going to run behind a man. I don't give a damn how good his dick game is.

"I can't believe I let you drag me on this double date," she said rolling her eyes at me. Vanity has been dating lately, but she finds an excuse not to go on a second or third date every time.

"He's tall, handsome and sexy. I think you will like him," I said smiling at her. She shook her head.

"Just remember to think short term. Don't go into tonight thinking about long term relationship goals. We just looking for someone to pop the cherry again. I think he might be the one," I said.

She laughed. "We?"

"I mean if you need me there to coach you through how to fuck, I'll be there for my sister by another mister," I said shrugging shoulders.

"You are too much," she said laughing.

SOUL Publications

I lifted the compartment between the seats and pulled out the packed foil. Here open this and get us one out. I had copped us some brownies to help her relax for this date tonight.

"What's this?" She asked taking the foil from me.

"Brownies," I said smiling at her.

She laughed. "I'm sure they are going to feed us Zelda."

I laughed. "Bitch, these special brownies." Her eyes grew big.

"I'm a doctor. I can't be doing drugs," she reminded me.

"It's not cocaine. Hell, that shit comes from the earth. It's not like you tending to patients tonight. It's Friday. You don't return to work until Monday. It'll help you relax," she said.

"If I become a drug addict, it's your fault," she said opening the foil.

I laughed. She passed me one of the brownies and took one for herself. She smelled it before pinching off a small piece. Her eyes widened when she realized they were

Dear, Vanity 2: Echon's Return   Nona Day

actually good. Before I knew it, she had eaten the entire brownie. I had to stop her when she reached inside the compartment for another one. I laughed as she sat in the seat relaxed as hell.

*****

"Oh, I forgot my phone," Vanity said as we walked inside the restaurant.

I turned to go back to the car with her, but she said to go ahead. I gave her the keys to go get her phone. A few minutes later, she joined me, Xavier, and Clyde, her date at our table. She was giggling uncontrollably. I shouldn't have let her eat the entire brownie. We all sat around making small talk as we ate. Clyde ordered us a bottle of wine. Vanity was throwing back glass after glass. I could tell by Clyde's facial expressions he wasn't feeling her behavior.

"Excuse us while we go to the ladies' room," I said standing up.

"You go ahead. I ain't gotta pee. I'm trying to find out what Clyde's dick gone do tonight," Vanity said smiling at him. Xavier nearly choked on the glass of

Hennessy he was drinking. Clyde stared at her with disapproval.

"Vanity, come with me," I said yanking her up.

I locked us in the restroom. "You shouldn't have eaten the whole brownie. You are acting a fool."

She bust of laughing. "I ate another one when I went back to the car. I feel so damn good. I'm going to fuck Clyde good tonight."

"Van, you are crazy? Those things are strong as hell. We are going home!" I demanded. The brownies and wine had her feeling herself too much.

"No, I want to have fun. Besides, those things got me horny as hell. Clyde bout to slide all up in these guts," she said trying to twerk off rhythm.

"We are going to go back out there and say good night. I'll explain everything to Xavier tomorrow," I said.

She pouted. "Whatever you say Mama." I shook my head as I led her out the door.

When we made it back to the table, the men were walking away. Being me, I looked down at the table. The first thing I noticed was they were leaving without paying the bill. I gave Xavier a mean stare.

Dear, Vanity 2: Echon's Return   Nona Day

"I can't believe you tried to fix my brother up with trash," he said. My blood started to heat up.

"Nigga, who the fuck you calling trash? My friend is a respected doctor," I stated angrily.

Clyde scoffed. "Well, she sure as hell doesn't act like it. She acts like she comes from the streets. I don't fuck ratchet hoes."

Vanity charged toward him to slap him, but I stopped her. "Nigga, I don't want yo square ass anyway. You better watch yo mouth before I make you disappear."

"Lose my number," Xavier said before trying to walk away.

I grabbed his arm to stop him. "That's fine by me but you gone pay this bill first."

"You're a lawyer. She's a doctor. You got it," he said with a smirk. I started cussing him out demanding he pay the bill. We had everyone staring at us, but I didn't care.

"What seems to be the problem over here?" A deep baritone voice spoke from behind me.

Dear, Vanity 2: Echon's Return   Nona Day

I quickly turned around to see who it was. I know it was management ready to throw us out. My breath nearly got caught in my throat. This brotha was the definition of delicious. He was tall, deep dark chocolate and sexy. His eyes were dark, his full lips were inviting, and his muscular body was causing a thud between my thighs. Everything about him was masculine down to the cologne he was wearing. His presence alone demanded respect and attention. I wanted to speak but my words was stuck inside the pounding in my chest.

"No problem. Just realized class can't be covered up with expensive clothes and red bottoms," Clyde said. The man gave Clyde and Xavier an ugly look.

"They invited us on a date. Now, they trying to leave without paying the tab," Vanity said walking up to him.

"Pay the tab or wash dishes," he said to them.

They chuckled until they saw the seriousness in his face. They reluctantly pulled out their black cards and gave them to the man. He nodded his head before walking away. Xavier mean mugged me as they followed behind him. I didn't care. His dick wasn't the best I had anyway. I turned around to make sure Vanity was okay. She stared at me before laughing out loud.

"Let's go," I said.

"Nope, there's a half a bottle of wine. You know our rule. Never go down on a unfinished bottle of wine," she said smiling at me. To be honest, I wasn't ready to leave. I was too intrigued by tall, dark and delicious.

Vanity

My head was pounding when I woke up the next morning. My mouth was dry like the Sahara Desert. I pulled myself out of my bed and made my way to the kitchen rubbing the sleep out of my eyes. My heart nearly leaped out of my chest when I saw Zelda laying in the middle of the floor face down with nothing but her panties on. She looked like she was dead. I rushed to her screaming her name. It felt like the weight of the world was lifting off my shoulders when she moaned.

"Please, don't scream Van," she said rolling over on her back.

"What are you doing on the floor?" I asked.

"I tripped and fell. I was too wasted to get home, so I just took my clothes off and slept here," she said sitting up. I laughed as I helped her get off the floor.

"Put on some clothes," I said walking in the kitchen.

She went to the spare room she usually slept in whenever she stayed over. She had more clothes here than she did at her own place. I grabbed the Tylenol bottle and popped three of them with a bottle of water. I finished the bottle without stopping. I grabbed another one and chugged it down. Zelda came in the kitchen and sat at the kitchen isle. She looked as if she was feeling the same way as me. I could barely remember what we did last night. The last thing I remember was sitting in the restaurant drinking wine after our dates ditched us.

"I've been going out since I was eighteen years old. Never have I got this wasted and acted a fool at the club the way we did last night. You was on one Van," she said massaging her temples. I passed her the bottle of Tylenol.

"What did I do?" I asked with worry.

"Don't worry. You didn't ruin your image. You was just having a lot of fun. Don't you remember going to the club?" She asked. I shook my head.

She laughed. "Girl, we had all the niggas feeling us. We were twerking our asses off."

My mouth dropped open. "Van we are professional grown ass women. We can't be out here acting like we still in college."

"Well, you should've thought about that before you gave your number to that lil young college student," she said smiling.

My eyes grew big. I don't remember any of that. Hell, I don't even know where my phone was. I sat down at the isle trying to remember last night's events. Everything started to come back. I covered my face in embarrassment. I was acting like a wild child. I was drunk and high as hell. I remember dancing on table tops and grinding my butt on some college kid. He couldn't have been no more than twenty-one years old. I even remember tonguing him down and getting my panties wet as we kissed.

"I can't believe I acted that way," I said shaking my head.

"The owner didn't mind. We got VIP passes for next Saturday," she said laughing.

"We will not be going," I assured her passing her a bottle of water.

"You have to admit it felt good to truly let go," she said smiling at me. It did but I will never tell her that. She would have me eating brownies and clubbing every night.

"Never again though," I stated. She laughed.

"God, I need to go brush my teeth and take a long hot shower," I said.

"What we doing today?" She asked.

SOUL Publications

Dear, Vanity 2: Echon's Return   Nona Day

"Recuperating," I said walking away.

"Well, I'm starving. Let's go out for brunch at least," she yelled as I walked into my bedroom.

I loved my bedroom. It was completely white the way Echon had his bedroom at his apartment. It was peaceful and relaxing. When I first moved in, I could still smell him. Now, all I smell is my perfumes and body sprays. I shook the memories from my mind and hopped in the shower. I stayed in until the water started to get cold. All I wanted to do was lay in the bed and get over this hangover, but I was starving. I slipped on a pair of burnt orange tights, a cream colored mid sleeve, button sheer blouse before stepping into a pair of tan four inch heels. I was walking in heels like they were flats now. I've walked in them so much now walking in flats felt uncomfortable. I was thankful I had a long, lace front wig on. It was a cinnamon color with rust colored streaks.

After applying a small amount of makeup, I searched for my phone. I started to panic when I couldn't find it. I needed my phone to check on EJ. I told him I would call him every morning at ten o'clock. I rushed down stairs. I breathed a sigh of relief when I saw it laying on the sofa. It was completely dead. I went to my study and put it on the charger.

"You ready?" Zelda asked walking in with her oversized, distressed jeans and an off the shoulder, light blue baby doll top. Her jeans were cuffed over her ankles and she rocking a pair of open toed, black stilettos that had to be six inches. She had her natural hair blown out and laying on her shoulders.

"Not yet. My phone dead. I need to charge it a little to call EJ," I said. She flopped down on the sofa.

She cleared her throat. "I didn't want to mention this but as your friend I have to. When we got home, you talked about him a lot last night. I know you'll never forget him, but last night was bad. I saw that sadness in you that I thought you had pushed through."

She wasn't lying. Lately, he's been on my mind more than normal. I don't know what it was but it's like I could feel his presence inside me. I remember a couple of weeks ago waking up gasping for breath because I had a dream of him dying in front of me.

Dear, Vanity 2: Echon's Return   Nona Day

"I don't know what it is. Lately, I can't get him off my mind," I confessed.

"Dick, you need some dick," she said seriously.

I rolled my eyes. "That's not it."

She shrugged her shoulders. "I know but good sex would help."

I laughed and shook my head. "I'm glad you didn't decide to be a doctor. Sex would be your remedy for everything." She laughed.

"Girl, this nigga been blowing my phone up all night," Zelda said looking at her phone.

"Who?"

"Xavier. That fool don't know me at all. He'll never lick this cat again. I'm on a whole new mission. I know exactly where we going to eat lunch," she said smiling.

The moment my phone came on I called Tree's phone. He picked up on the first ring. I could tell by his voice he was worried. I apologized for worrying them. They were actually getting ready to fly here to see what the problem was with me. He gave EJ the phone and he talked nonstop about how much fun he was having with everyone. I ignored the numerous notifications coming through my phone as I enjoyed listening to his stories. After we ended our call, I checked my phone. I had numerous texts and calls from an unknown number. When I read the texts, I realized they were from the young boy I almost had sex with. I erased them all and blocked his number.

"Young Thug blowing up yo phone?" Zelda asked smiling at me. I shook my head.

"Let's go. I'm starving," I said ignoring her question.

Echon

I couldn't stop running on the treadmill. I knew I couldn't run to the place I wanted to be but, just the thought of being there wouldn't let me stop. I thought of her every day. I wondered did she hate me, was she happy, and if she found someone deserving of her soul. I tried not to let anger consume me when I thought of someone loving who I still felt belonged to me. I regretted I never sent her the letter I wrote her. I know she feels I chose murder and living in my own hell over her. I always thought I was strong enough to defeat anything, but I was far from right. Trying to forget and stop loving her was a losing battle. I prayed like a man raised on the belief in God from birth. Every day and night I talked to God for the strength to let her live the life she deserved. I never returned to Atlanta. I knew if I ever laid eyes on her I wouldn't be able to walk away. So many times I was tempted to reach out to Quran to get an update on her, but I knew it was best I didn't. I know he would talk me into returning. Now here I am stuck in a place not knowing where, why or how I got here. I was breathless and sweat poured down my body as I continued to try and run from the ache in my heart. The last thing I remember before waking up in this place was being shot numerous times in a parking lot. Going by what they tell me that was three years ago. Two of those years I was in a coma. Since I woke up all I've done is workout, read and think about her and the family I grew to love. I didn't even have a picture of her. I didn't need one anyway. Her beautiful face and soul was engraved in my heart, mind and soul.

"You can run as much as you want. That treadmill ain't taking you anywhere," the short, stocky, dark skinned nigga said walking in the exercise room. I couldn't stand his ass. All I know is his name is Thomas. I already whooped his ass last week for talking too much shit. The only thing stopped me from snapping his neck were the security that was guarding me. I still haven't met the person who saved my life and was keeping me hostage.

"Shower and get dressed. Dinner will be served in an hour," he said.

I stopped the treadmill and stared at him. "Nigga, when have I ever sat down and broke bread with you?"

He chuckled. "And believe me the feeling is mutual. You will finally be meeting the man that saved your life."

For the first time he said something that mattered to me. I didn't know if I wanted to kill or thank whoever it was that was keeping me held here. I got off the treadmill

Dear, Vanity 2: Echon's Return   Nona Day

and walked out the room. I couldn't deny how anxious I was about dinner. Ever since I awakened, I've been asked to be released from the big beautiful mansion. All everyone would tell me was I would meet him in due time. The mansion was heavily guarded with militia men. I knew one false move from me and they wouldn't hesitate to kill me. The French Renaissance style mansion was sitting on many acres of beautiful green grass. There was an enormous grape orchid and building behind the mansion where wine was made every day. I didn't care for Victorian style décor in the bedroom, but I couldn't deny how comfortable the bed was. The black canopy styled bed looked like some shit Batman would sleep in.

I took a long cold shower and got dressed. I needed a haircut and shave. I didn't care about getting either. All I wanted was to go back to live my life and possibly a life with her. I don't know how but I'm going to make it happen. I made my way downstairs. I didn't know where the dining room was because I always ate in my room. Shavonna was making her way toward me as I searched for the room. Shavonna was one of many women that frequented the estate. She was a short, thick and black mixed with Puerto Rican. She made it obvious she wanted to fuck me. All she's gotten so far is my dick in her mouth.

SOUL Publications

I was a man and my dick spoke what my heart and mind didn't sometimes. I could count the number of times I've had sex since I left Atlanta. I felt like fucking another female was cheating on Vanity.

"You looking for the dining room?" She asked smiling seductively at me.

"Yea."

"Follow me. He's waiting for you," she said turning around and walking away.

I had to admit she was built like a stallion. Her ass jiggled as she walked in the short tights she wore. She reminded me of the rapper, Nicki Minaj. Thinking of music made me think of Tree. He had me listening to all types of music. Most of it was trash though. I wondered how he was doing. I saw great expectations in him. He was hungry, fearless and a great observer just like me. I was surprised when she took me to a small dining room. I expected to walk into one of those with high ceilings, chandeliers, and a long table that sat about forty people. The small room had a table set for two people.

"Have a seat. He'll be here shortly," she said nodding toward the table. I walked over and sat at the table.

"And Atsu if you need company tonight, I'm available," she said.

Who the fuck is Atsu? I thought, but I didn't ask.

A tall man with my skin complexion walked into the room. He was an average looking man with a neatly trimmed low afro. He looked to be in his mid-fifties. Shavonna dropped her head. He told her she may look up. She smiled at him like he was her savior. He leaned down and kissed her lips before dismissing her. Damn, if that's his woman she ain't shit.

"Sorry to keep you waiting," he said still standing. My only thoughts were how could I kill him and get the fuck out of here alive. I remained quiet. I didn't have anything to say that he wanted to hear. I wanted to hear everything he had to say.

"She's one of my wives. They are here to satisfy your every need as they do mine," he said smiling.

"Nah, one is enough for me. So if we can get this dinner over, I can get back to her," I said.

"I know you've been asking for my presence since you awakened. I wanted to give you time to fully recover. We have a lot of things to discuss," he said.

Dear, Vanity 2: Echon's Return   Nona Day

"A year is plenty of got damn time. Why the fuck are you holding me here? Who the hell are you?" I asked angrily standing up.

"There's no doubt you could kill me with your bare hands in this room. The only problem is you wouldn't make it pass the door before you are killed," he said confidently.

My eyes scanned the room without moving looking for another exit. There was one way in and one way out. I didn't have guns to shoot my way out of the damn room.

"Sit down," he nodded toward my chair.

"Mothafucka, you sit down. I prefer to stand," I said. I don't give a damn who he was. I wasn't bowing down to him.

He chuckled. "Fearless and strong." He sat down at the table and looked up at me. I sat back down across from him.

"It's good to see you at your full strength. When we first brought you here, I didn't know if you were going to make it," he said.

"Who tried to kill me?" I asked.

Dear, Vanity 2: Echon's Return   Nona Day

He cleared his throat. "I don't know. I found you after years of searching for you after Zuberi's death. When I finally found you, you were in a hospital as John Doe. They couldn't find any records of who you were."

"Why were you looking for me? And who is Zuberi?" I asked.

His glared at me. "Zuberi is your father. I'm your blood Uncle. My name is Kasim."

As long as I can remember I always wondered if any of my family was still living. I would lay in the bed at night asking myself if they were searching for me. All I knew was my parents were dead, but I searched for extended family members for years. After unsuccessfully finding anyone I gave up. I sat there staring at the man with my heart pounding and mind racing. I had so many questions. The first one was if he was telling me the truth, but I was speechless. I don't know if I wanted this to be true or not. I didn't know how much this could possibly change my life.

"I know you are in shock. Here's what I'm going to do. I'm going to walk out of here to give you time to gather your thoughts and feelings. When you are ready to talk…come to me. I will answer all of your questions," he said standing up.

He walked to the door and turned to face me. "It's good to have you home, Atsu." I didn't like him calling me that name. I don't know Atsu. Guap was the armor that kept me strong. Echon is the man that found love and happiness in this cruel world. Echon is who I am.

Two Days Later

Echon

I hadn't slept all night. She made me believe in having a happy and bright future. Now my past came with a face attached to it. He could tell me everything I always wanted to know. Everything in my gut was telling me to leave the past in the past. My mind wanted to know who I truly am. Usually I ran on the treadmill every morning. Today was different. Something inside me felt different. I thought of Sam Cooke's *A Change Is Gonna Come*. I felt change deep inside me. I didn't like the feeling I was having. It felt like a raging storm. I decided to go out for a morning run. Of course, I couldn't go alone. I guess my uncle knew I wouldn't come back if I went alone. I had three guards trailing me in a Hummer as I jogged down the long deserted road. I was being held in Raleigh, North Carolina. There were no houses in sight. There was only trees and the highway for miles.

When we got back to the house, a white Ferrari with cream colored interior was parked in front of the mansion. I searched the house until I found Kasim in the outside jacuzzi with two of his women. He smiled up at me.

Dear, Vanity 2: Echon's Return   Nona Day

"Good to see you, Nephew." The more I looked at him I saw so many of my own features in his face.

"I'm ready to talk," I said to him.

"Good, get cleaned up and meet me in the main study. You can take one with you if you like," he said with a wink. This was one of those times my dick was telling me to get one of them, but my heart and mind said don't do it. I walked away without replying.

After taking a cold shower, I went to the main study. The tall walls were lined with dark brown oak bookshelves. The furniture was beige with black and brown designs. The floors matched the dark brown bookshelves. He sat behind the tall, executive styled desk. I walked over and sat in the chair in front of the desk.

"Why am I here?" I asked.

"We will get to that later. First, I want to tell you about yourself," he said sliding over a picture album.

I don't know why I was so nervous. I sat there stiff as a board staring at the book. I slowly took the book from the desk and opened it. On the first page was a picture of a beautiful chocolate woman and a man that was no doubt

Dear, Vanity 2: Echon's Return   Nona Day

my father. It was their wedding picture. They looked to be
no more than twenty-one. All I could do was stare at their
picture. They looked happy and in love. I finally tore
myself away from their picture and turned the page. On the
back of the page was two newborn babies. It was obvious
they were twins. A flood of emotions took over me. Joy,
sadness, pain and love filled my heart all at once as I
continued to flip through the album. My parents took so
many pictures of us as a family. I always wondered what
kind of parents I had. Now, I know. I had loving parents. I
have a twin brother that I never knew about.

"You were only two years old when you were taken
from them by Kylo," he said. Kylo was the name of the
man that raised me as his son.

"Taken?" I asked confused. Kylo always told me he
found me in a dark alley.

"Let me tell you about your parents first. We will
get to him later," he said. I nodded my head. I wanted to
know everything about them. I can't remember anything
about them, but I felt their love by looking at all the
pictures of us.

Dear, Vanity 2: Echon's Return   Nona Day

"Your father was sent to America with an elderly rich white man when he was only twelve. His grandfather wanted a better life for him than what he had in Africa. His parents were killed by some racist white men. He was already in love with your mother at that age," he said smiling.

"The white man was a good man. He gave Zuberi the best life," he said.

"What was my mother's name?" I asked.

"Asha," he answered.

"The white man died leaving everything he owned to your father at the young age of eighteen. He was a head in a powerful drug cartel. All of this belongs to your father which means this is all yours," he said looking around. I didn't give a damn about any of this. I wanted to know what happened to my parents and brother. He could keep all this shit as far as I was concerned. He continued with his story.

"Your father returned home to wed your mother. They returned to the states as husband and wife. They had a great life. They were so excited when they found out they were pregnant with twins. Life was perfect for them until the older heads of the cartel started turning their businesses over to their children. Some of the children decided you had to be a part of the bloodline to be in the cartel. If not, everything was taken from you. Your father wasn't a man to bow down to anyone's rules. He decided to fight for everything that was his. The young leader of the cartel came in with an army one night and killed them. I found your brother, Jabari in the woods near the house. I searched for you for years. I couldn't find a trace of you or Kilo. I assumed you were both dead. I didn't found you until Kilo knew he was dying. He sent me a letter telling me what he did. He confessed to setting your father up for money. He thought he could right his wrong by raising you to be a soldier like your father," he told me. All of the emotions stirring inside me turned to hate and rage. I wanted to dig his ass up and kill him again.

"Why didn't you reach out to me after his death? Where's my brother?" I asked.

"Your brother died a few years ago," he said dropping his head. I knew my parents were gone, but I was overjoyed to know I had a blood brother. I could feel water filling up in my eyes. I closed my eyes tight to hold back the tears.

Dear, Vanity 2: Echon's Return   Nona Day

"You were a nameless man. It took me years to find you after his death. When I finally did…" he said shaking his head.

"What?" I asked.

He stared at me. "When I found you, you were working with the enemy that killed your parents." I gave him a puzzled look waiting for him to explain.

He sat up straight and stared me in the eyes. "Basilio Vega's father is the one that ordered the execution of your parents."

All the darkness returned inside of me. He was still talking, but sounding far away. So many questions were running through my mind. My head started to pound along with the adrenaline pumping through my heart. I felt a feeling I hadn't felt in a long time. I felt the need to kill.

"I know this is a lot to take in. I'll give you some time to let it all soak in," he said attempting to stand up.

"No!" I asked angrily.

He slowly sat back down. "Murdoch, the white man that raised your father was smart as hell. He had enough evidence to take down the whole cartel. That's why they killed your father. They couldn't risk him snitching if he walked away. Your father left all the info in a safe which I found. I walked away with everything that belonged to your father except his place in the cartel."

"And what was his place?" I asked.

"He was supposed the be the head of all families," he said.

"What happened to my brother?" I asked through gritted teeth.

He cleared his throat. "After I found you, I wasn't sure if I could come to you with what I knew. You were loyal to the enemy. You were like his shadow. It's hard for someone like you to turn your back on someone you considered family. So, I watched you from afar. Just waiting for the perfect time. I know Bull was in the middle of a war, so I sat still. My men were trailing you the night you were almost killed. Me and your brother wanted revenge for your parents' death. He agreed to take your spot as Bull's shadow. The plan was for Bull to get everything he wanted and take it all from him like he did your father. Your father was building a militia to protect his family. Ever since they died, I spent years continuing to build that army to take him on. Bull is a strategic man. Taking him down isn't easy. Killing him doesn't give us back what is rightfully ours. We have to take over the cartel that he now owns and runs. Your brother was killed in a shootout fighting with him in a takeover. He died protecting the son of your parents' murderer."

"Why the fuck did you let him go in as me?" I barked jumping up out the chair.

"It wasn't my choice. We had only discussed him taking your spot. I knew he needed to be mentally and emotionally prepared. He wasn't ready for the task. Your brother made the decision without me. After we brought you here, he went missing. He didn't give me time to strategize. I thought he was dealing with the emotions of finding his long lost brother. He appeared a month later and told me he stepped in as you. It was a brilliant plan, but I think the role he took on became a reality to him. He truly became you…a protector," he tried explaining.

Dear, Vanity 2: Echon's Return   Nona Day

"This folder is everything you need to know. It collaborates everything I just told you. It's time we take back what belongs to you. He is living your legacy," he said sliding the manila envelope toward me.

The last time I saw one of these it caused me to walk away from the woman that made me enjoy living. Now, one of them is causing me to want to destroy the man I grew to love as family.

A Month Later

Vanity

"You decided if you're going to New Orleans with us after EJ gets out of school?" I asked Zelda as she worked behind the bar.

I had just come from another date with a nice guy named Emmanuel. We've been dating for the past three weeks. I actually enjoyed his company. He was tall, brown skin, nicely built and a perfect gentlemen. He owned his own security company. We've went on a few dates and I'm really started to like him. I'm just not trying to move too fast. Every time I try to move forward memories of Echon come flooding back. I know I have to let him go. I have got to stop trying to find the love we shared in every man I date.

"I don't know yet," she said dryly. For the past couple of weeks Zelda haven't been acting her normal hyper self.

"You've been acting funny for the last couple of weeks. What's going on with you Zee?" I asked her.

Dear, Vanity 2: Echon's Return   Nona Day

"I don't know Van. I'm ready for a change in my life but every guy I meet is the same. I'm starting to think a lot about love and a family. Having spontaneous mind-blowing sex with fine ass big dick men with no emotional connection has gotten old," she said.

She walked off to serve a couple of customers that approached the bar. I was shocked to hear her talk this way. Zelda loved living her life carefree. She never wanted to fall in love. She felt it was overrated. Me on the other hand felt like life was meaningless without love. We went back to the restaurant looking for the sexy, dark skinned man that she had her eyes on, but he was never there. She finally gave up. She walked back over to the bar and looked at me.

"I even started back fucking Xavier," she said shamefully.

I cringed. "Why?"

"Because I'm familiar with him. I wanted to feel someone I was connected to, but I realize we never had a connection just mediocre sex," she said.

I walked behind the counter and poured both of us a shot of Jack Daniels. She laughed. "So, you trying to turn up turn up." I laughed with us.

Dear, Vanity 2: Echon's Return   Nona Day

A couple of hours later, we were both dancing to the old school music. The lounge only played the oldies. We wanted to keep the vibe grown and classy. I was in my zone swaying my hips to the sound of Marvin Gaye's *Sexual Healing* when I felt a pair of strong arms around my waist from behind. It felt good being held in his arms. I leaned back against his broad chest.

"I got home and couldn't stop thinking about you," Emmanuel whispered in my ear.

I turned around to face him. He was definitely handsome. He licked his sexy full lips as he stared at me. I wrapped my arms around his neck and pulled his head down to meet my lips. The bulge in his trousers started growing and pressing against my stomach. For the first time, I kissed a man without thoughts of Echon. We spent the rest of the evening dancing, drinking and talking. Zelda even approved of him. I didn't want to rush things with him, so I declined his offer for a nightcap at his place.

After me and Zelda locked up the lounge, it was after three o'clock in the morning. I crashed in one of her spare rooms. EJ was staying over at Quran's mother's house. I woke up remembering today was Sunday. I

Dear, Vanity 2: Echon's Return   Nona Day

promised him I would take him and a couple of his friends to Six Flags today. I decided I wanted to visit a church before going. I wasn't a member of any congregation. I decided to let my heart lead me to visit whatever church I wanted to. I didn't feel the need to join a particular church. Just like God was in all our hearts, he was in all churches. At least he's supposed to be. I wonder about that having visited a few churches though. I went upstairs and woke Zelda up. She hated going to church, but I was dragging her with me today.

Few Hours Later

I sat in the pew amused at what I was about to witness. This was a holiness church, so I knew it would be eventful. I just never imagined Zelda would be a part of it. The pastor called for anyone that wanted their souls cleansed to come to the front of the church. I was shocked when Zelda stood up and walked to the front of the church. My stomach was cramping as I sat there trying not to laugh out loud looking to the front of the church. The pastor started prophesying to each person. He would then pour a dab of holy oil on their head and say a prayer for them. Each member would start shouting and speaking in tongues until they fell out on the floor. I sat anxiously waiting for

Zelda's turn. She looked so nervous and scared. The pastor started telling her that God wanted her to give her life to him in order to receive the blessings she wants. He dabbed oil on her forehead and prayed for her. Zelda didn't do like everyone else. She just stood there waiting for the Holy Ghost to hit her. I snickered when I almost laughed out loud. Her eyes met mine and she pleaded for help. I shrugged my shoulders.

"Child, you are full of demons. We have to cleanse you of the evilness inside you," the pastor said pouring more holy oil on top of her head.

Still nothing happened to Zelda. He called the deacons to join him in praying for Zelda. They all joined hands and circled around her while praying for her. The pastor continued to bless her with more than enough oil. After a few minutes, Zelda busted out of the middle of their circle. She came rushing down the aisle.

"Let's get the fuck out of here," she said glancing at me as she rushed out of the double doors. I stood up and raised my one finger and walked out behind her.

Dear, Vanity 2: Echon's Return   Nona Day

When I got in the car, she was sitting in the driver's seat fuming with rage. Her long expensive weave was soaked with oil as well as her Donna Karan dress. I finally released the laughter I was holding inside.

She started to cry. "I'm evil. They couldn't even get the demons out of me."

I reached over and wrapped my arms around her. "No you are not."

"Well, why didn't I do like the rest of the people?" She asked breaking our embrace.

I snickered. "I can promise you half of those people faked it. Zelda, there's no certain reaction to feeling God's love inside you. I've never acted like those people when I feel the Holy Spirit inside me. I remember the first time I felt it. A pastor's words felt like they were coming directly from God to me. I sat in the pews with tears running down my face with a feeling of complete peace and joy inside my heart. Sometimes I sing loud when I feel His Holiness inside me. Don't force it. You'll know when you feel it."

She looked down at her ruined dress. "Look at me. I can fry a pan of chicken with all this oil." I bust out laughing.

She reached over in the glove compartment and pulled out a blunt. "You can't smoke that now. We are taking EJ and his friends to Six Flags."

"That's exactly why I need it after that fiasco. Is Khalil lil perverted ass going?" She asked. I laughed. Khalil had a big crush on Zelda at eight years old. His big brown eyes stayed glued to her ass. She lit the blunt while still parked in the parking lot at the church. We both jumped when someone tapped on the window.

"Oh shit, that's one of the deacons," she said staring at me with wide eyes. I snickered while she held the blunt. She let down her window.

"I just wanted to come check on you," he said to her looking at the blunt in her hand.

"Thank you. I'm fine. Just needed something to relax me," she said nervously.

He looked back at the church. "Mind if I hit that?" I laughed. She shrugged her shoulders and passed him the blunt. He got in the back seat and started spilling all the tea about the pastor. He was sleeping with several women in the congregation. He said he only came to this church because the women are freaks. Before we pulled off, they

Dear, Vanity 2: Echon's Return   Nona Day

exchanged phone numbers to set up a date. I love my best
friend.

SOUL Publications

Zelda

I was exhausted after spending the day at Six Flags. All I wanted was my bed, but here I was driving to a hotel to meet Xavier for a drink on a Sunday night. I stopped letting niggas come to my place. Half of them didn't know when to leave. All I wanted them to do was make my body feel like a cooked noodle and go home. Well, that's how I used to think. Lately, I've been wanting more. I just know Xavier wasn't the one I wanted it with. I stopped dating hood niggas since I was representing so many in court. Seeing wives, girlfriends and baby mamas worried if their men are going to be sent to prison made me realize I didn't want to end up with one of them. I only dated corporate now. But damn, I miss the rough, shit talking, hair pulling, ass smacking, choking sex from a hood nigga. I pulled up to valet parking and gave them my keys. Just as I was walking inside the hotel bar, a text message came through. I exhaled in frustration as I read Xavier's excuse for ditching me when he was the one that set this up. I decided since I was here, I might as well have a drink.

I sat at the bar and ordered a lemon drop martini. I know I had to drive home, so I couldn't have the double shot of Tequila I so desperately wanted. I almost dropped

Dear, Vanity 2: Echon's Return   Nona Day

the martini glass when he walked through the door from behind the bar. I stared up at him waiting for him to recognize me. He never looked my way. He walked over to the bartender and started talking. I waited anxiously until he was done. He walked pass me only giving me a head nod. I became slightly agitated. I may not be the best looking or finest woman he's seen but I'm not fucking forgettable.

"Excuse me," I said loud enough to stop him in his tracks. He turned to face me. Damn, he is sexy as fuck.

"I'm sorry. How can I help you?" He asked.

"You work here too?" I asked. He squinted his eyes like he was trying to figure out who I was.

He walked back over to me. "Do I know you?" I was embarrassed that he didn't remember me when I've been stalking the restaurant looking for him.

"I met you at the restaurant. You made the men pay for me and my friend's food," I reminded him.

"Oh yea, you look different," he said.

I remembered I was wearing a long curly weave that night. Today, I was wearing my natural hair. "Might be

Dear, Vanity 2: Echon's Return   Nona Day

the hair." He nodded his head. I've never been nervous around a man before, but this one had me feeling insecure.

"You need another drink?" He asked.

"Yea, a double Tequila," I said. I needed something to calm my nerves. He poured the shot and sat it in front of me.

"You're not going to join me?" I asked.

He chuckled. "Naw, I'm on the clock."

He walked back into the office without saying another word. I was losing my touch. I downed the shot and called the bartender over for another. I waited for him to come back out of the office, but he never did. I was drunk and horny. I was too wasted to drive home, so I got a room at the hotel. I didn't want to bother Van. It was a school night and she was home with EJ. I ordered some fast food through UberEATS since the restaurant inside the hotel was closed. I went to my room and took a shower. I slipped on the robe since I didn't have any sleepwear with me. I don't know what was wrong with me. I wasn't feeling like my usual self. I thought getting closer to God would help, but that's not the issue. I know my relationship with God. I was trying to fix something that wasn't broken. Maybe I should try being celibate. Yea, that's what I'll do. I'll spend some

Dear, Vanity 2: Echon's Return   Nona Day

time loving myself. Forget a man and sex. I said to myself.
I was happy when someone knocked on my door. I was
starving. My heart dropped when I opened the door. He
was standing there holding my bag of food from
Smashburger.

"Thank you," I said snatching the food from his
hand.

He chuckled. "You're welcome. You gone invite
me in?" As much as I wanted to, I decided against seeing
was he as good as he looks.

"No, you should've gave me the attention I wanted
when I was interested," I said trying to close the door.

He held his hand to the door and stopped it from
closing. He stepped inside without my permission. He
smelled so damn good. He pulled at my robe tie causing my
robe to fall open. I gasped in disbelief as my bag hit the
floor. I immediately closed my robe.

"Get out," I said angrily.

He laughed and picked up my bag from the floor.
"Come sit down and eat."

Dear, Vanity 2: Echon's Return   Nona Day

I don't know why I was obeying his orders. I followed behind him like a little whipped puppy. We sat at the small table and he pulled my burger and fries from the bag. When he licked his full lips my pussy jumped.

"Eat your food," he ordered. Like a dummy, I did what he said. He sat texting on his phone while I ate.

"You can leave now," I said.

"I'll leave when I'm ready to go. What's your name?" He asked.

"I don't like you enough to tell you my name. Either you get out or I will call the cops," I said angrily. I hated that I still wanted his rude ass.

He slid his chair back from the table. I was relieved he was finally leaving, or so I thought. "Come here," he said staring at me as if he wanted the very same thing I wanted.

It was like he had me under some kind of spell. I didn't even know his name, but I was obeying his every command. I stood up and walked to his side of the table to stand directly in front of him. He pulled the tie on my robe and I let it fall open. My breathing became shallow as I waited for him to do whatever he pleased with me. So much for being celibate. He gently grabbed me around the waist, lifting me up and sat me on the table. He pushed my legs apart exposing my shaved pussy.

"You got a fat pussy and you soaking wet," he said staring at it. I was embarrassed. I tried closing my legs, but he held them apart. He leaned in closer and inhaled deeply.

This was stupid. I've never let a man control me this way. I pushed his head from between my legs. "You need to leave."

"You don't have a scent," he said.

I jumped off the table. He was rude as fuck. I know he wasn't the one I wanted to give my love to. He was a complete asshole. "I know nigga. My pussy don't stink. Now, get out. I thought you were worth fucking but I was wrong."

He laughed as he stood up. "I don't fuck strangers anyway. Maybe that's something you should try. Ain't nothing sexy about a thirty year old thirst trap."

Before I knew it, my hand was going across his face. He wrapped his hand around me and pulled me into his chest while his other hand was wrapped around my neck. I didn't know if he was going to kill me or rape me. I can't say it would be rape because my pussy was dripping wet for him. He stared down at me with a scowl on his face. The next thing I knew our tongues were having a fighting match inside each other's mouth. I have never craved a man the way I did him. I started sweating and breathing heavy as we tongued each other down. I pulled his shirt over his head. His dark chocolate body was ripped with muscles and abs. Just when I started to unbuckle his pants my phone rang. Normally, I would have ignore it, but it was the ringtone I had just for Vanity. I broke our make out session.

"I have to get that," I said trying to catch my breath. He nodded his head. I rushed over and grabbed my phone. I know something had to be wrong. It was almost midnight. Vanity is usually asleep at this time.

"What's wrong?" I asked.

"I'm okay. I just had a bad nightmare. I was hoping you could make me laugh to forget about it," she said sadly.

"About Echon?" I asked. For the past few months, she's been thinking and dreaming about him a lot. She was doing so good at one time. I don't know what's causing the setback.

"He was standing in a field covered in blood. He was calling for me, but I couldn't reach him. There was a sheer dark aura surrounding him," she said. I could feel the hurt in her voice.

"I'll be over in thirty minutes. We'll watch Friday. You know you love that movie," I said making her giggle.

"What other movie you know that made millions with one setting? They made millions with just about the entire movie being made on the front porch. And you know I've always had a crush on Chris Tucker," she said laughing. I laughed with her.

"Hang up and cook us some breakfast," I said. I only took a bite of my burger, so I was still starving. I turned around to let…damn, I still didn't know his name. Anyway he was already gone when I turned around.

Vanity

It's been a couple of weeks since I had the dream of Echon covered in blood. Some nights I dreams about him, other nights are nightmares that leave me crying until I fall asleep. I was ready for vacation. Two weeks to get my mind together. Maybe visiting his grave will make me feel better. I don't know what happened. I was loving life and happy. All of a sudden, it's like the earth shifted and brought back all my sadness. I've canceled two dates with Emmanuel this week. I truly liked him. I wanted to see where things would go between us. He wanted to come over last night, but I wasn't ready to have him at my house with EJ here.

Today was a day for relaxing. I had a hard depressing week at work. It was one of those weeks where I had to send a parent to a specialist only to receive what I know was going to be bad news about their child. One more week and I will be stress free for a couple of weeks. Me and Zelda was lounging by the pool while Quran grilled for EJ and a few of his friends. I was watching EJ and his friends play in the pool. He's getting so big. I wish Echon could've at least got a chance to see him. I tried setting Quran and Zelda up on a date. Neither one was interested. I thought they would've made a cute couple. Zelda was in a daze as she scrolled through her phone.

"You okay?" I asked her.

"Yea, I just need some back breaking sex," she said bluntly.

I laughed. "It's hard being celibate."

"Bitch, hard ain't the word. How do you do it?" She asked.

I shrugged my shoulders. "It was easy before Echon because I didn't know what I was missing. Now, it's hell since he's the only one I want it from."

"Well, give Emmanuel some. You aren't being unfaithful to him Van. It's okay to love someone else," she said.

"I know. I was thinking about surprising him tonight. You think you can watch EJ for me?" I asked.

"Yes! I want all the details tomorrow," she said excited.

"Tomorrow is Sunday. Are we going to church again?" I asked smiling at her.

"No, that shit ruined my damn expensive ass weave," she said angrily. I laughed.

Dear, Vanity 2: Echon's Return   Nona Day

"Yea, Vanity told me you got baptized with the Holy oil," Quran said catching the end of our conversation.

"Yea, mothafuckas were flapping around on the floor like fishes out the water," Zelda said. Quran rolled in laughter.

"Y'all can come to church with me. My friend goes to a nice Methodist church," he said.

"Oooohh, Uncle Q gotta girlfriend," EJ said walking up trying to high five Quran.

"Boy, go back out there in the pool. Stay out of grown folks conversation," Zelda told him.

"But we thirsty Aunt Z," he said.

"When the hell you start calling me Aunt Z? What happened to Tee Tee?" She asked.

He laughed. "Tee Tee is for babies. I'm becoming a man."

We all laughed as he stuck his bird chest out. "Get the rest of them. It's time to eat anyway."

"Quran you could've invited her over," I told him.

Dear, Vanity 2: Echon's Return   Nona Day

"She had to work today," he said blushing. I was happy he had someone in his life. He is a great man that deserves someone that can love him the way he deserves.

The boys stayed outside to eat while we went inside and sat in the kitchen. We all looked at each other when my doorbell rang. I never had unexpected visitors. People were starting to move in the neighborhood, so I assumed it was a neighbor. When I looked at the security monitor, I was shocked to see Tree and Yella Boy standing outside. I immediately went to welcome them inside.

"I'm sorry to intrude, but we looking for Zelda," Yella Boy said. I was confused. Him and Zelda could barely stand each other.

"Yea, she's in the kitchen, I said leading them. After introducing them to Quran, Tree went outside to see EJ.

"Yella Boy wants to speak with you. We'll give you some privacy," I said looking at Quran.

"Naw, you good but I don't know him like that," he said looking at Quran.

"He's EJ's Godfather," I told him.

"Like I said, I don't know him like that," he repeated. I was used to the way he talked. Not everyone understands his way of communicating. Quran chuckled and dismissed himself.

"Must you be so damn rude? And what could we have to talk about?" Zelda asked him.

"I'm not rude. I'm real. Ain't you a lawyer or something?" He asked her.

"There's no such thing as or something. I'm either a lawyer or not," she stated. I prayed they weren't in any trouble.

"Well, is you?" He asked.

"Boy, I don't have time to go back and forth with you. What the hell do you want?" Zelda asked frustrated. Celibacy was not working out for her. She was short of patience and mean. I laughed.

"Twelve got my cousin last night. Our lawyer is on a damn cruise ship. I need someone to get him out," he said.

"I don't do pro bono," Zelda said with a smirk. She knew Yella Boy had money. She just liked getting under his skin.

Dear, Vanity 2: Echon's Return   Nona Day

"You gone go to the damn jailhouse and see him or what?" He asked.

"Now?" I asked surprised.

"Yea, she's his lawyer. They'll let her see him," he explained.

"What is he in for?" She asked.

"Drugs," he said bluntly.

They went back and forth with questions until she finally agreed to go see him. She called to get a visit, but they were still processing him. She informed them she would be there tomorrow to see him. He thanked her with a couple of stacks of bills. I know it was at least twenty-thousand. She graciously declined.

"I talk shit with you but as long as Van looks at you as family, you are my family also. Like it or not." She licked her tongue out at him in a childish manner. He chuckled.

"You a'ight too Zero," he said walking away.

"My damn name is Zelda," she yelled as he kept walking.

Later That Night

Dear, Vanity 2: Echon's Return   Nona Day

I know I was taking a chance showing up to Emmanuel's house unannounced. We are supposed to be exclusive, so it shouldn't matter. If there is someone here, I'll know he wasn't the person for me. I felt like I've been pushing him away. I didn't want to do that. I wanted him to know I was serious about building a relationship with him. I took a deep breath before knocking on the door. When he opened the door with nothing on but a pair of boxer briefs, I couldn't help but stare at his print.

"What's wrong Vanity?" He asked with concern.

I didn't know what to say. I knew why I was there, but the words wouldn't come out. I wanted closure. I was ready to move on with my life. I will love Echon with all my heart for as long as I live, but I couldn't let his memory keep me from living my life. I came prepared for what I wanted. With nothing under my tee shirt dress I stepped inside. His confused eyes stayed on me waiting for a reply. I just stood there trying to figure out my next me.

"Vanity, talk to me. What's going on? Is EJ okay?" He asked. He was a good man. The type of man that I could love. He was what I needed in my life. Those were the words I said to myself to go through with this.

Dear, Vanity 2: Echon's Return   Nona Day

When he closed the front door, I pushed him against the door pressing his back against the door. I placed my hands on the sides of his face and pulled it down. I covered my mouth with his. He groaned at the pleasure of me sucking his tongue into my mouth. I started kissing, licking, and sucking all over his neck and chest. I slid my hand inside his boxers and stroked his rock hard rod.

"Damn Vanity, you sure you ready to do this?" He asked. I didn't want to think about his question. If I thought about it, I know I'll change my mind.

"I don't want to think about it. I want this," I said seductively.

"Fuck! You don't know how bad I want you," he moaned as he started licking and sucking on my neck. When he slid his hand under my dress, he realized I didn't have on any panties. He stopped and stared at me.

"You came ready I see," he said smiling at me. I stepped back and pulled my dress over my head.

He licked his lips as his eyes roamed over my body. "God, you are beautiful."

Dear, Vanity 2: Echon's Return   Nona Day

He stepped to me and lifted me up. I wrapped my legs around his waist. His kissed me as he walked me to his bedroom. He laid me in the middle of the bed and looked down at me. His body wasn't like Echon's, but he was in shape. *Stop it Vanity! Don't compare them!* I screamed the words in my head as he stepped out of his boxers. He pulled me to the foot of the bed and kneeled down between my legs. My body started to heat up. I could feel the wetness forming between my thighs. He started licking and sucking my inner thighs. My womanhood started pulsating and begging for some of the same attention.

When his wet tongue lapped across my lower lips, chills went through my body. I moaned in ecstasy when his tongue dipped between my wet slit. He spread my legs resting the soles of my feet on the bed. His moans and groans became louder and louder as he licked and slurped my wetness as it poured from me. Feelings of guilt clouded my mind until he flicked his tongue over my swollen bud. I clamped my legs together locking his head in place. He sucked on my bud and my essence poured from me. My screams and moans echoed through the room. My body shivered and jerked as I squeezed my legs together even tighter.

Dear, Vanity 2: Echon's Return   Nona Day

After I came down from my blissful high, I released his head. He stood up licking his lips with my juices dripping from his goatee. He slid on a condom as he stared down at me. I scooted back up until I was in the center of the bed. I spread my legs apart inviting him inside of me. He lay on top of me holding his torso up by placing his hands on the bed. He studied my face to see was I ready. I was ready. I raised my legs wrapping them around his waist. He started licking his way down to my breasts as I stroked him with my hand. I could feel the thudding of his member against my inner thigh. His tongue made wet circles around my dark areoles. My flower started opening up when he bit and sucked on my nipples. I placed him at my entrance to enter me. He slowly started sliding inside my wet tunnel. It wasn't painful, but my tightness needed to adjust to him. He laid his torso on top of me. He whispered sweet nothings in my ear as he glided farther and farther inside. That fiery feeling inside my soul wasn't there. I couldn't close my eyes, because all I saw was Echon. I stared up at the ceiling wondering was this a mistake. He gave me slow, deep, and loving strokes as his tongue licked and sucked my neck. I felt an orgasm coming so I became wild. My hips bucked and gyrated. I dug my nails into his back as I prepared for my body to explode. He

Dear, Vanity 2: Echon's Return   Nona Day

pushed deep inside me and my essence squirted between us.

"Fuuuuccckk Vanity!" He roared as he sped up his pace. He barked and groaned about how good I felt as he started ramming himself inside me harder, deeper and faster. Sweat started pouring from his body as he continued to give me every feeling my body had been craving.

He pulled out and flipped me over on all fours. I regretted letting him make that move the moment I looked back at him. I was so caught up in the moment I forgot what was on my lower back. Echon's name was tattooed on my lower back in cursive letters with hearts and rose designs around it. It's the only tattoo I will ever have. I could see the hurt in his eyes as he stared at it. I could only give him a sympathetic glance. He slid back inside me giving me slow deep strokes. As deep as he was, I still needed him to go deeper. I bucked trying to get him to hit those spots that haven't been touched in years. Before I could get another orgasm, he exploded inside the condom. His body jerked until he collapsed beside me.

"I love you," he whispered in my ear. I wanted to say it back, but I couldn't. Not right now. Hopefully, eventually I will be able to say those words to him.

Dear, Vanity 2: Echon's Return   Nona Day

I stood up to go to the bathroom. Something didn't feel right in the pit of my stomach. He's gone. I don't understand why I feel as if I just cheated on him. I felt I needed to take a shower to wash the betrayal from my body. I know in my mind I didn't do nothing wrong, but my heart was telling me otherwise. I went back to lay in the bed beside him.

"This is the beginning of something beautiful," he said pulling me in his arms. I laid my head on his chest knowing I didn't feel the same way.

"The tattoo?" I asked.

"We can get it covered," he said. I didn't think I could. Well, I know I can, I just don't know if I want to do that.

Next Morning

Zelda

"It's about damn time," Yella Boy said when I walked into the room. I was running late. This celibacy shit has my body out of whack. My patience and nerves are shot. I wasn't in the mood for his insults. They wouldn't let me see him yesterday, so I had to wait until today to meet him. I hadn't even looked up his arrest.

I gave him a stare. "Not this morning. Don't come for me."

"What's wrong with you?" He asked as I placed my briefcase on the table and flopped down in the seat across from him.

"Just not a good morning," I said.

"Well, thanks for doing this on such short notice," he said looking away.

I smiled. "You're welcome."

"The fuck you smiling at me for?" He asked grilling me. I laughed and shook my head. He wasn't a bad guy. His mouth just has no chill.

"What's your fiancé like? She has to be slow as fuck to deal with you," I asked. He ignored me and started scrolling through his phone. A few seconds later, he slid his phone over to me. A picture of a beautiful slim thick sister with a boy cut was on the screen.

"She's beautiful," I said looking up at him.

"She's going to school to be a psychiatrist. My mouth was worse before her," he admitted.

"Awww, you're in love," I said smiling at him. He tried not to blush, but his face started turning red. I thought it was so cute that he couldn't hide how he felt about her. He chuckled and shook his head.

We sat chatting until the door to the small room opened. I couldn't believe who was coming through the doors. It was him. The nigga that has taken over my dreams. Ever since Vanity's call interrupted us from having sex, I couldn't stop thinking about him. He wasn't the clean shaven guy that I met. He looked like the sexy ass hood niggas that I was addicted to during my college years. Even in the orange jumpsuit, he still made my heart pound.

"Oh hell no! I know this isn't your cousin," I said jumping up staring down at Yella Boy.

He glanced at me and then his cousin. "You two know each other?"

His cousin chuckled. "Yea, we've met a couple of times."

"Sorry, I can't take this case. I'll recommend a lawyer for you," I said grabbing my briefcase.

"Guess you going back to your cell," the officer said that accompanied him.

Yella Boy stood up. "Look, just represent him in the bond hearing. My lawyer will be back next week."

When I glanced at him, he smirked and winked at me. There was no way I was taking his case until I gazed at Yella Boy's desperate eyes and the racist ass cop. I had no proof he was racist, but the spirit of my ancestors inside me told me he was a racist. That's all the confirmation I needed. I placed my briefcase back on the table and took a seat. The officer uncuffed his wrists. He smiled at me as he massaged his wrists. Everything about him made me nervous. He gave Yella Boy a brotherly hug and they both sat across from me. I could feel his eyes on me. I could barely stop my hands from shaking. I forced myself to go into lawyer mode. One thing I was sure about was that I was a damn good lawyer. I asked all the questions I needed to know to prepare for court. He answered all of them without making any smart remarks. I guess he saw how

Dear, Vanity 2: Echon's Return   Nona Day

seriously I took my career. I learned his name is Jedrek

Barnes. Everyone calls him Drek. After we were done, the

officer escorted him out to be transported for the court

hearing.

*****

About an hour later, I was sitting in the courtroom

waiting for my client and the judge. I wasn't concerned

about getting him bail. I knew the judge very well. He was

an older married man that has been trying to fuck me since

the first time he saw me. I don't fuck married men, but he

doesn't need to know that until after I get Jedrek out on

bond. If he tries to revoke his bond, I'll gladly show his

wife all the text he sends me begging for sex.

Jedrek came through the side doors with an officer.

When he sat next to me, I tensed up. He didn't smell like

cologne, but his masculine aroma was like an aphrodisiac.

He looked rugged and sexy in the orange jumpsuit.

He leaned over and whispered in my ear. "You got

my dick hard."

My eyes immediately went to his crouch. I dropped

the folder in my hand when I saw his massive hard dick

laying on his thigh under the jumpsuit. I fumbled with the

folder when I leaned down to pick it up. I regretted wearing the low cut blouse, because his eyes were focused on my breasts. The blouse was only meant to entice the judge.

Almost two hours later, I was standing outside the courtroom with Yella Boy. For a minute, I wasn't sure if the judge was going to grant bail. I had to give him a few seductive glances to persuade him. I stayed around long enough to make sure he was processed for release. The moment I knew he was being released I hauled ass. I hated the way he made me feel but loved it at the same time. He was the type of man I wanted to stay far away from. He probably got a few crazy bitches stalking him and baby mamas he still fucking.

Later That Night

"So, what was it like?" I asked Vanity as we lounged in her den drinking wine. I didn't want to go home to my empty house, so I came to stay with her. Plus, I was anxious to know about her night with Emmanuel.

"It was good," she said uncertain.

"But not stalker good?" I asked.

Dear, Vanity 2: Echon's Return   Nona Day

"I mean it probably could have been, but…" she said shrugging her shoulders. I knew it didn't have the effect on her that Echon had.

"But you couldn't stop thinking about him?" I asked.

She glared at me. "I had to force myself to not think about him. He was giving me everything he had, but something was missing. I felt so guilty afterwards."

"Van, you have no reason to feel guilty. You have to move on. I'm sure the feeling will pass the more you have sex with him," she said.

"I hope so. He's a good man. I do care a lot about him. He saw the tattoo," she said nervously.

"You let him fuck you from behind before telling him about it?" I asked surprised. I told her to let him know she had Echon's name tattooed on her before they had sex.

"I got caught up," she said.

"So, it was at least good enough to make you forget about the tattoo," I said.

"Not exactly. I was so caught up into trying to feel that feeling that he gave me. No matter how hard he gave it to me or how much I gave it to him, I couldn't get that soul binding sexual feeling," she said.

Dear, Vanity 2: Echon's Return   Nona Day

"Damn, soul binding. Shit, I've never felt that," I said.

"When we had sex, it felt spiritual. I know that sounds crazy but it's the truth. It's a feeling that's hard to explain, but you will know it when it happens. I remember he could stroke his fingertips across my body and I felt like I was going to explode between my thighs. The way he would look at me made me want to give myself to him wherever we were," she said reminiscing.

"You're not helping with my celibacy talking like that," I told her. She laughed.

"I've never really discussed Echon with him. He only knows EJ's father died. I know seeing the tattoo lets him know exactly how much he meant to me," she said.

"Talk to him. He needs to know his competition isn't a threat," I advised her. She nodded her head.

EJ came into the den rubbing his eyes. "EJ, what are you doing up?" Vanity asked him. He was looking more like his daddy every day.

"I had another dream about my daddy," he said. My eyes grew big. Vanity told me she's been having dreams and nightmares about Echon. She never mentioned EJ was having them.

"Come here," she said reaching for him. He walked over and sat beside her. She wrapped her arms around him.

"You don't have to be scared. Your father would never harm you," Vanity said.

"I know Mama. We were playing football in the back yard," he said smiling up at her. I could see the tears forming in her eyes as she held EJ tight. A few minutes later, EJ went back to his room.

"They started a few weeks ago with him," she said referring to EJ's dreams about Echon.

"Nightmares?" I asked.

"No, always happy dreams," she said smiling.

Before closing my eyes that night, I prayed Vanity finds someone who gives her the love she deserves.

One Week Later

Echon

I was going home today. I have so many mixed feelings. The thought of seeing her face again was a mixture of happiness and nerves. The thought of seeing the man that I considered a brother was filled with anger and sadness. My first choice was to return to her, but seeing her would be a distraction. I needed answers from Bull. I didn't want to return to her with the hate that was inside of me. Bull was like my brother. I can't believe he knows what happened to my parents. The betrayal I felt in my heart made me want to kill him instantly. I didn't give a damn about taking over his organization. None of that meant anything to me. My only concern was vengeance for my parent's and brother's death. My uncle's only concern was taking back what was rightfully ours.

"I can't let you go alone. Basilio is a guarded man. It would be too dangerous for you to walk in there all alone," my uncle said as we walked out of his study.

"I've been protecting myself since I was a child," I told him.

Dear, Vanity 2: Echon's Return   Nona Day

"But you've never faced men like him alone. Trust me, he's not going to give you what belongs to you so easily. Killing him won't get it back. This has to be an orchestrated takeover," he said.

I turned to face him. I didn't want him making any moves until I said so. "You said all this belongs to me. So, I demand nothing is done without my say so."

He gazed at me as if he was trying to read my thoughts. He nodded his head and continued to walk. I didn't know how I was going to confront Bull. I know I could easily catch him off guard. As far as he knows I'm a dead man. I wanted to look him in the eyes and hear him tell me he didn't know about my parents. If not, he will be a dead man. I could care less about what happens to the business.

"Your father's empire has dwindled tremendously over the years. Basilio's empire has taken over most of what he controlled. Most of the wealth remaining is in properties. You and your brother are supposed to be wealthy and powerful men. His father took that from you and gave it to his children. You need to keep that in mind," he stated eyeing me with cold vengeful eyes.

"I could never forget the life I was forced to live for so many years," I reminded him.

He nodded his head. "Follow me."

I walked behind him deep in my thoughts until we entered the huge garage. It was big enough to hold at least fifteen cars. He stopped when we stood in front of the only car that was covered.

"Your father loved this car. It's only right you have it," he said pulling the cover from the car.

I instantly fell in love with the all black 1963 Dodge Charger. He placed the keys in my hand. It felt good owning something that my father loved. I've been spending time learning as much as I can about him and my mother.

"Thomas will accompany you with a few soldiers," he said.

"Nah, I'm good. I don't like that nigga," I told him.

"He's family. He's for your protection. He will keep his distance. He'll be the eyes you need to cover your back," he informed me. I didn't have time to argue with him. As long as he kept his distance from me, I didn't care where he went.

Dear, Vanity 2: Echon's Return   Nona Day

Few Hours Later
New Orleans

It felt strange being here. Everything looked the same, but felt so different. I wasn't the same person that left here. I know my life wouldn't be the same. I felt it in my soul. I wondered what it would be like seeing her for the first time. I wanted to forget going to see Bull, and drive to Atlanta. I decided against the idea since Thomas and his men were traveling behind me. I didn't want them to know anything about her. We checked into our rooms. It felt surreal using my government name. We arrived in the middle of the day. I was ready to go get the answers I came for. Thomas and his boys wasn't going with me on this visit. This was between me and Bull. I took a nap until the sun went down. I didn't realize how tired I was. I woke up after ten o'clock that night. I slipped out the hotel without them knowing.

I drove to Bull's estate with different intentions than when I initially got on the road coming to New Orleans. Being here changed something inside me. I didn't feel the hate I felt when I was in Raleigh. This was a place that showed me nothing but love after leaving Vanity. Whatever happened in my past made me the man I am today. I realized sometimes God lets things happen in your life to prepare you for the future. My future was with her. If my past hadn't happened, I would have never met her. No amount of hate could overcome the love I have for her. Nothing was worth jeopardizing losing a second chance with her.

I still remembered the layout of the estate like the back of my hand. Until I spoke to Bull face to face, I couldn't trust anyone. I decided to break into the mansion without anyone seeing me. It was almost midnight, so only a few security men would be canvasing the yard. I slipped inside the mansion with ease. The mansion was completely redecorated. I made my way to the study where Bull spent most of his time.

"Basilio, don't be down here too much longer," Worth said. I immediately slipped out of her sight when she opened the door.

"I won't Bella. I'll be up shortly," he said.

I waited until she disappeared from the long hall. I couldn't ignore the nerves in my gut. It wasn't fear. I was anxious to see him. Bull had become like a brother to me. We learned a lot from each other over the years we worked together. I was overjoyed to see him, and Worth get the

Dear, Vanity 2: Echon's Return   Nona Day

happy ending they deserved. I know there was no way I could destroy that when they fought so hard for their love. I took a deep breath before opening the door. I stood there staring at him. He never looked up from the computer screen.

"Bella, I said…," he starting speaking before looking up to stare me in the eyes.

He sat there like he was seeing a ghost. This was the first time I saw a bit of fear in him. He couldn't move. He sat there with his mouth slightly opened just staring at me. I stood there holding my gun elated to see my brother. I walked slowly to his desk. Neither of us had spoken a word. I know he had so much running through his mind, but was too discombobulated to speak. He slowly started to stand as I walked closer. The closer I got I saw just how much this moment affected him. His eyes were full of tears. He walked from behind his desk. We stood face to face with each other. He studied my face to see was it actually me.

"It's me," I said.

He wrapped his arms around me for an emotional brotherly hug. Whatever animosity I felt for him for what his father did, didn't matter. This will forever be my brother. I hugged him back relieved to be back home with my family. We stood there for several minutes just embracing each other. I know this moment was far more emotional for him. For the past few years he thought I was dead. All of a sudden, he started laughing hysterically. For whatever reason, I started laughing with him. He finally broke our embrace.

"Man, I got so many damn questions," he said staring at me.

"I know. I'll explain it all. First, I need the truth from you," I said. I didn't want to waste time. I needed to get this all out the way and get to her.

"About?" He asked.

I stared him in the eyes. I didn't want to see him blink when I asked him about my father. I needed to see that he wasn't hiding the truth from me. Whatever his answer was didn't matter. I wasn't seeking revenge. I just needed to know my brother didn't lie to me for years.

"My father," I said.

He squinted his eyes as if he was trying to understand what I was asking. He took a step back. Before he could open his mouth to speak the double doors to the study slowly opened. Thomas stepped inside and put a single bullet in Bull's chest. He stumbled back on the desk and slumped down on the floor. Blood was spreading over his shirt rapidly.

"Mothafucka!" I barked raising my gun at Thomas. Two of his men stepped in behind him pointing their guns at me.

"Kill me and you die with us. We got about a minute before security comes in here. We triggered the alarm in the garage," he said staring at me with a smirk. He turned and walked out with his men.

I couldn't leave him here to die alone. I stood over him as his life slowly slipped from him. Just as I was about to lean down to help him Worth came barging in the study. She looked down at Basilio's body. The screams that came from her were gut-wrenching and painful to hear. She charged me and started throwing blows that landed on my face and chest. I grabbed her by her arms and shook her.

"I know this shit is crazy, but I need you to pull it together if you want him to live," I said staring at her. She glanced down at his body. She cried harder when he coughed up blood.

"He's dying," she said pulling from me and leaned down by his body.

"Worth, I need your help!" I barked at her. She was distraught. She saw the same thing I saw. His life was seeping from him on to the floor. She stood up and wiped the tears from her face.

"What do I do?" She asked with so much hurt in her eyes.

"Call 911. I need the sharpest knife you have, bandages, and towel now," I said. She glanced at him one more time before hurrying out of the room.

I kneeled down beside him and tore his tee shirt down the middle. I pulled mine from over my head and wiped the blood from his chest. I was relieved to see the bullet hole was farther right from his heart. He was still losing too much blood. I pressed my tee shirt to his chest to stop the blood. Worth came rushing back inside with her

Dear, Vanity 2: Echon's Return   Nona Day

arms full. She dropped everything on the floor and kneeled down beside Bull. She informed me 911 were on the way.

"He's going to feel this pain, but it won't be too bad. I need you to hold his hand and talk to him to keep him calm," I instructed her. She nodded her head nervously. She leaned down and whispered in his ear. I cut a small incision into his chest to see where the bullet was. It was too deep for me to pull out.

"The bullet was too deep inside. It's too deep for me to dig out. I need to elevate him. Use the towel to keep pressing on his chest. He doesn't need air getting into it. It'll collapse his lung," I informed her. I got behind him and sat him up. I sat behind him with his back against my chest to keep him elevated. I didn't want to chance carrying him to the sofa. She cried and pleaded with him to fight for his life. He coughed causing blood to spew all over her. She screamed when he lost consciousnesses. He wasn't breathing. I laid him down.

"Worth, I need to do CPR," I said as she cried as she held on to him.

"Pleas save him," she pleaded with me. She moved out the way. She kneeled beside me praying as I tried to bring him back. I was silently praying with her as I pumped his chest.

"Tilt his head and breathe into his mouth," I told her.

"I know how to do it," she informed me. We repeated CPR a couple of times before he coughed just as the paramedics came rushing inside. I breathed a sigh of relief and stepped out the way, so they could assist him. Sheba and Dose rushed into the study. Their eyes met mine. She fainted. Dose caught her before she could hit the floor. The cops rushed to me putting me in handcuffs.

New Orleans

Vanity

We had arrived in New Orleans this morning. We were unpacking at the penthouse Worth had reserved for us. EJ wanted to stay with Tree. Since Zelda came with us, I thought it was best we stay in a hotel. It's not like I was worried anything inappropriate would happen. I just felt Nika didn't know Zelda well enough to invite her in her home with her husband. Zelda wanted to stay in the penthouse also.

"Giiirrrll, you gotta see my suite," she said busting in me and EJ's room.

"It ain't bigger than ours," EJ said excited.

"It's not," I said correcting his English. He was definitely picking up a lot of things from Tree and his friends.

"It sho ain't," Zelda said looking around.

"How can he speak proper English when you are a lawyer and says sho?" I asked glancing at her.

"Right. Key words…I am a lawyer. He'll be fine. We are," she said winking at me. I just shook my head.

SOUL Publications

"I'm surprised Worth isn't here. She said she would be here to welcome us," I said.

"Girl fine as her husband is, she probably still home hunching," she said in a low voice so EJ couldn't hear. I laughed.

"I'm going to call Nika and let her know we are here," I said grabbing my phone. I called her number, but it went straight to voicemail. Tree's phone did the same thing. I tried calling everyone's number, but no one was answering. I started to worry.

"It's still early. Maybe they are still asleep. Let's go down to the restaurant and have some breakfast. We'll try and call them later," Zelda said. I forced a smile and nodded my head. The nervousness in my stomach told me something was wrong.

Zelda went back to her room to take a shower and change. After unpacking, showering and getting dressed we made our way down to the hotel's restaurant. The hotel was absolutely exquisite. It was nice enough for top celebrities. The food and service was five stars and more. EJ kept asking when we were going to his Uncle Tree's house. I was pulling out my phone to call Nika when her and Zuri walked into the restaurant. As happy as I was to see her, I didn't like the look on her face. EJ jumped out his seat and rushed to them giving them a hug.

"Do you have a feeling something is wrong?" Zelda asked me as Nika and Zuri approached our table.

"Yea," I said dryly.

I stood and gave them a hug. I introduced Zelda to Zuri, since they had never met. EJ immediately started asking to go to Nika's house. They joined us at the table. I know nothing could be wrong with Tree or Yella Boy or they wouldn't be here.

"Is everything okay?" I asked nervously.

"Zuri is going to take EJ to Lamar's house where Baby Gladys is. Is that okay with you?" She asked ignoring my question. I had met Lamar on previous visits. I know I could trust him with my son.

"Yea, that's okay. He need to pack a bag?" I asked. She nodded her head. We all went back up to my room to gather his things. A child's innocence to the world is everything. EJ was ecstatic about his trip. Me on the other hand was a nervous mess. I know something was wrong. After getting everything packed for him, Zuri said she would meet up with us later. She gave Nika a hug and left with EJ.

"Now, are you going to tell us what the hell is going on? Is Bull and Worth okay?" Zelda asked.

"Vanity, I don't even know how to say this. We better sit down," she said walking over to the couch. I don't know why but I couldn't move. Zelda grabbed my hand and led me to the couch.

"This is all like a unbelievable dream and horrible nightmare," Nika said shaking her head.

"Tell us what the nightmare is," Zelda said. I couldn't speak. My adrenaline was pumping to my heart rapidly causing it to pound in my head.

Tears started to fill Nika's eyes. "Bull was shot last night. He's in a coma fighting for his life." She sobbed softly wiping the tears that slid down her cheeks.

"Oh my God! What happened? Where's Worth and the kids?" I asked finally breaking my silence.

"The kids are with her mother. Worth is at the hospital with everyone else," she said. I know there was more to the story.

Dear, Vanity 2: Echon's Return   Nona Day

"Did they get who did it?" I asked. She dropped her head for a few seconds and looked up at me again with so much sorrow it frightened me.

"Who did it?" Zelda asked.

"Echon," she said in a low voice.

"It sounded like you said Echon. What did you say?" Zelda asked her. I didn't need to hear her say it again. I saw it in her eyes. My head was spinning, heart pounding, and my body heat skyrocketed.

"He's alive Vanity. I saw him with my very own eyes. The police have him in custody for questioning," she said staring at me. My throat started closing up. I started taking short, deep breaths. It was like all the air was being sucked from me. I started hyperventilating.

"Get her some water please Nika," Zelda said as she stroked my back. I guzzled down the water when Nika gave it to me.

"Breathe Van," Zelda said trying to calm me down. Tears started to fall. I didn't know if they were tears of joy or pain. How could he be alive and not come back to me and his son? Why would he only resurface to kill Bull? Where has he been? Questions rushed through my mind as I started pacing the floor.

Dear, Vanity 2: Echon's Return   Nona Day

"I know this is a lot Vanity. I wish I had the answers. We didn't get a chance to talk to him. To be honest, we're not sure if he even shot Bull. Worth walked in and saw him standing over his body with a gun in his hand. He performed CPR and saved him. That's all we know," Nika said.

I grabbed my luggage and started throwing all my clothes inside. I needed to get away from all of this. He's supposed to be dead. He's not supposed to come back into my life and break my heart all over again.

"Take me to get my son. I'm leaving," I said as I threw clothes in the luggage.

"Van, calm down," Zelda said grabbing my wrist.

"Calm down my ass! I have cried for that nigga every day since he walked out my life, only to feel like I was dying on the inside when I found out he was dead! Now, he comes back. Not to see me or his child but to kill more people! No! Fuck him!" I screamed.

"Are you sure it's him. This doesn't make sense. I thought he was buried in his grave," Zelda said to Nika.

Nika shook her head. "I don't know who is in that grave. I looked in that man eyes tonight. It is Echon."

Dear, Vanity 2: Echon's Return   Nona Day

"I don't give a damn who he is! I want my son! I'm leaving!" I yelled at them.

Zelda walked over to me and snatched the luggage from my hands. This was the Zelda that didn't take no shit and took control. She was over my behavior and I knew it. "Van, where you gone run to? Running back to Atlanta ain't gone make this go away. That is EJ's father. Even if you don't want to see him, he deserves the chance to meet his father. We don't know what happened to Bull. You have to calm down and find out. If it's him, you have to deal with his return. Now, suck it up got damn it!"

"I have to get my son. He may be in danger. Maybe it's someone after Echon. They might know about EJ," I said pulling away from Zelda.

"Lamar's house is guarded like the White House. No one is going to harm him, but if it makes you feel better, we'll go get him," Nika assured me.

I wiped my tears. "He doesn't need to see me this way. I'm a mess. Promise me he'll be safe."

"I promise," Nika assured me.

Zelda

So much for a relaxing, stress free vacation. This crazy fool would decide to be Lazarus while we're here on vacation with his son. We had just arrived at the hospital. Everyone was sitting around the room quiet. My heart broke for Worth. Her bloodshot eyes were filled with worry and pain. I noticed the blood seeped into her clothes as Paisley sat beside her trying to keep her calm. Dose, Fila and Sheba's eyes were filled with worry and anger. Tree and Yella Boy's eyes were consumed with confusion. I know everyone was wondering what happened. My heart dropped when Jedrek walked into the room. This nigga was out on bond and wasn't supposed to leave the state. Well, he wasn't my concern anymore. I did my part. He walked over and whispered something in Tree's ear. Tree gave Dose and Fila a head nod. They all walked out the room. Sheba walked over and sat on the other side of Vanity.

"You doing okay?" She asked her.

"I'm so sorry," Vanity said looking up at her. I guess she felt she was responsible for Bull getting shot. Only Vanity would think that way.

"You have nothing to be sorry for. You didn't do this. We don't know what happened. Worth doesn't even know. All we know right now is he saved Bull's life. The cops took him in before we got a chance to talk to him," Sheba explained.

"I can't believe he's alive," I said.

"That's how we all feel. There's so many questions. He's the only one that can give us answers but our concern is Bull right now," she said.

Zuri walked in the waiting room kneeling down in front of Vanity. "EJ's safe. He's in the backyard playing the Baby G and Fiji." Vanity nodded her head.

"You want anything to drink?" Zuri asked Vanity while Nika helped Paisley console Worth.

"No thank you," Vanity said.

Yella Boy stepped back into the room and asked me to step out in the hallway. I looked at Vanity to make sure she would be okay. She told me to go ahead. All the men were standing around with heavy minds.

"We need you to go down to represent him," Yella Boy said.

Dear, Vanity 2: Echon's Return   Nona Day

"Oh hell no you don't! Y'all are fuckin millionaires. Don't tell me you can't get him a lawyer. Hold up, why would you even want to get him a lawyer?" I asked glancing at all of them.

"He's requesting you. No one else," Jedrek said staring at me. I stood there speechless. *How did he even know I finished law school?*

"You either go in there and find out what happened to Bull or he's dead by morning," Dose warned me. The thought of Vanity having to go through his death again was too much.

"Fine," I said reluctantly.

"Drek will take you," Yella Boy said.

"No he will not. He's not even supposed to be out of the state of Georgia. I'm not riding dirty with a criminal," I said staring at him.

He stepped in my space. "I guess you better make sure I stay out of trouble while I'm here." This man was my weakness.

"Now I have to go back in there and explain this to Van," I said.

"Just gone. I'll explain it to her," Tree said.

"Don't tell her where I went. Just make up some shit," I told him. I walked away and stood waiting for the

Dear, Vanity 2: Echon's Return   Nona Day

elevator doors to open. I could feel him standing behind me. He was so close his dick was poking against my ass.

"I can't wait to fuck you," he whispered in my ear. I hurried on the elevator when the doors opened. I was relieved people were on it with us. I probably would've been fucking him on the way down to the main lobby.

Police Precinct

Jedrek wasn't allowed in the room with me. I sat nervously waiting for them to bring Echon inside. I jumped when the big steel door opened. I quickly stood up. I wanted to stare him in the face. I needed to be as close as possible to him. He walked through the door and we glared at each other. Anger instantly took over. I walked over and slapped him hard across the face for all the pain he's put Vanity through. Not one muscle in his face twitched. He stood there like a statue. It was like he wanted me to slap the other side of his face. I gave him what he wanted.

"That's enough!" The officer demanded. I backed away and sat down at the table. He sat on the other side. The moment the door closed behind the officer I cussed him out with everything I had in me. I was so angry I didn't realize I was crying. My anger was mixed with joy to see him alive. This was definitely Echon.

"How is she?" were the first words to come from his mouth.

"I'm not here to update you on her or speak on her behalf. I'm here because you requested me as your lawyer. All we need to discuss is what happened to Bull," I stated firmly.

"Is she happy?" He asked ignoring everything I said.

I leaned over the table and got in his face. "I'm not telling you a got damn thing about her. Your concern right now should be your own life. They want your head for what happened to Bull. If you did it, you are dead for sure this time. Now, you need to tell me what happened before they try to arrest you. Arresting you will put your prints in the system. I'm sure I don't have to remind you have your previous career. You don't want the chance of those prints showing up anywhere."

"How's he doing?" He asked showing his concern for Bull. I could tell by the look in his eyes it was genuine.

Dear, Vanity 2: Echon's Return   Nona Day

"He's in a coma fighting for his life," I informed him.

"I didn't do it," he said. I felt the relief take over my entire body. There was so much we had to discuss. The first thing was getting him out of here. I banged on the door for the officer.

"How did you know I finished law school?" I asked.

"I wouldn't expect anything less from you. Just like I'm sure she's some kind of doctor," he said. If only he knew the half of what she was. She was the mother of his child. He finally opened the door with a scowl on his face. *Racist ass pig.* I thought in my mind.

"I need to speak to the detective in charge of this case," I stated. He turned and walked away. The detective came back in the room a few minutes later.

"What is your reason for holding my client?" I asked.

"He's a suspect and witness to an attempted murder. He was carrying a gun. That's reason enough," he said.

"Does the gun match the ballistics that was taken from the victim? And is the gun registered?" I asked.

"We're still waiting for the results," he said.

"Well, until the results show that it was his gun we are done here. Don't worry we won't leave town," I said smiling at him. He walked out the door slamming it behind him.

"Let's go," I said looking back at Echon.

We rode back in dead silence. I texted Nika and told her to get Vanity away from the hospital. This wasn't the time for the reunion. His life was still in limbo. He has four angry ass men waiting for him. There wasn't a drop of fear in his eyes. He's got to be some special kind of crazy. I glanced over at Jedrek. He stared down at my thighs. All I wanted to do was ride his dick until kingdom come. Damn, he is sexy. We pulled in front of the hospital.

"Take my car back to the hotel. I'll come get it later," Jedrek said.

"I don't know where I'm going."

He punched the address of the hotel in the GPS. "Now, you do."

Echon stepped out the car with me. I grabbed him by his arm. "I don't know what happened at the house, but you better have some answers for them. If not, you know what they will do."

"You seem concerned about me," he said smiling at me. Me and Echon started off on shaky ground. I wasn't sure of his intentions with Vanity. Once I saw how much he loved her, he was my brother. We argued like siblings.

I glared at him. "This is no time to be grinning and shit. Your life is on the line. She knows you are alive damn it. Don't let her have to go through you dying again."

His eyes brightened up and widened. "Where is she?"

"Save your fuckin' life first. Then, you come find her. She's going through all kinds of emotions right now," I told him. He has no idea the surprise he has waiting for him.

SOUL Publications

Echon

There was no way Zelda got to New Orleans that fast. I had only been at the precinct for a few hours before she showed up. I don't even know how she knew I requested her as my lawyer. For her to come so soon, she had to already have been here. If she was here, I know Vanity was here also. I had so many questions running through my mind. What were they doing here? How did Zelda know one of Bull's men? Those were the most important questions that were pounding in my head as I walked with the tall, dark skinned brother down the hospital hall. I know I should be scared for my life, but I know I didn't shoot Bull. I was guilty of unknowingly leading the man to the house that did shoot him.

When we walked into the room, Fila and Dose stared at me with rage and shock. Tree and Yella Boy were staring with a mixture of emotions. I didn't know Yella Boy that well, but I watched him hustle when Tree brought him in. I always thought he was a peculiar acting dude. Dose is the next in charge after Bull. So, I gave him my attention. He stood up and walked over to me. He studied my face to see was it truly me. After realizing it was, his fist met my face. I took the blow I felt I deserved. I wiped

Dear, Vanity 2: Echon's Return   Nona Day

the blood that dripped from my bottom lip. He jacked me up by my shirt and pinned me against the wall.

"Yo, we can't do this shit here," Fila said standing up. Just when I was getting ready to speak my peace, Dose's phone rang. He let me go and looked at the screen. I could tell by the look on his face the call was important. He stepped back and walked out to the hall.

"I don't know where the fuck you been or what you've been doing, but you better start talking," Fila warned me.

"I wouldn't be here if I tried to kill him. If I wanted him dead, he would be. You know that," I said.

"What the fuck happened in there?" He asked.

Before I could answer, Dose walked back into the room. He charged toward me punching me in the face again. This time I knew it wasn't going to be just one punch. We started throwing hard jabs at each other. We tied up and wrestled each other to the floor. We were trying to overpower each other as we tussled on the floor. He gave me a hard jab to the rib cage almost knocking my breath from me. The blow I gave him to the throat caught him off guard, but didn't stop him. The others stood around and watched us tear up the waiting room. We didn't stop until security came. We were all escorted outside the building by security.

"What was that all about?" Tree asked Dose. He was raging man.

"While this mothafucka was trying to kill Bull, his team took over our cocoa fields in Columbia. They've taken out our entire team we had guarding the fields. They've raged a street war on some of our territory," Dose said gazing at me with fiery eyes. Everyone stared at me with the same eyes. I had no parts in what went down, but my actions led to everything that has happened.

"I didn't try to kill Bull. I damn sho didn't order anyone to take over his fields or territory," I said glancing at all of them. Police cars pulled up in front of the building.

"Take his ass to my house. Don't let him out your sight," Dose demanded.

"I have no intentions of running," I assured him. He walked away.

"I'll take him," Tree said never looking at me. We walked to his car without saying a word to each other. I

Dear, Vanity 2: Echon's Return   Nona Day

watched Yella Boy hop in his car with the dark skinned guy.

I could tell Tree was uncomfortable with me in the car. I could see his chest going in and out. He was holding a lot in. I know there was plenty he wanted to say. I decided to break the ice.

"I never faked my death. I didn't come here to kill Bull or take over his organization," I informed him. He cut his eyes at me, but didn't speak.

"Who da fuck did we bury? Where have you been?" He asked angrily.

I shook my head. "This like some soap opera shit. I was shot before everyone thought I was dead. I was in a coma for like two years. The past year I've been held in some big ass mansion by my uncle."

He quickly turned his head and stared at me with wide eyes. Tree thought I didn't have family the same way I've thought all my life. "Yo Uncle?"

I nodded my head. "Yea." As he drove, I told him everything I learned from my uncle. With everything that has happened, he's the mothafucka I want to kill. I told him

I didn't want any actions from him or his militia until I said so.

"Man, this shit don't make no sense. Why did he need you to do all this?" He asked.

"I don't know, but I'm going to find out," I said.

He turned his head to look me in the eyes. "You telling the truth."

"I've never lied to you about anything. There are some things I withheld about my past, but I've always been real with you. I respect you too much to lie to you," I told him.

"You think Bull knew who you was?" He asked.

"The moment I mentioned my father, he was shot. Honestly, I don't think he did. When I left the mansion, my focus was on getting revenge for what happened to my parents. When I hit the city, everything changed. I remembered my life here. Building a bond with everyone and prayer is the only thing that kept me sane."

"You pray?" He asked.

I chuckled. "Privately."

"I met her." I didn't have to ask who her was, I knew. I just stared at him. I never told anyone about

Vanity. It was my way of protecting her from anyone in my past or future.

"That shit fucked me up when you died. It took me a year to go through your house. When I finally did, I found the letter and phone in your safe. I had Genius find out who the number belonged to. I thought it was a family member. I found her and took her the letter. When I told her you died, I felt like I was living your death all over again. She was fucked up bad," he said shaking his head. I hated the thought of her thinking I was dead. I can't imagine what she went through.

"I never wanted to hurt her," I told him.

"You coming back is probably hurting her more right now. She's been trying to move on with her life," he said.

I raised my brow at him. "You saying I should've stayed gone?"

He stopped at the light and gave me his full attention. "I'm saying if you aren't ready for what she needs, you should've stayed gone. Don't take that as me wishing you was dead. My heart bout to fuckin' bust from sitting here with you in this car. I want you here. I just don't want you coming back to tear her down. She's fought too hard for the moments of happiness she has in life."

I held my hand out for him to shake it. I needed to know he understood me. I wasn't here to cause anyone harm. I only came back for peace and her. He locked hands with me. I pulled him in for a brotherly hug.

"You think she hates me right now?" I asked.

He chuckled. "Nigga, if minds could kill people, you'd be dead right now. She thinks you tried to kill Bull. You came home to murder instead of coming home to her."

"Well, get me to Dose's house so I can state my case. I need to make sure I'm not a dead man walking before I step to her," I said.

He chuckled. "It's good to have you back."

I nodded my head. "It's good to be back. And look at you. Nigga, I always knew you would be running your own empire. Your hustle was serious. You still fucking with Hemi. I never liked that nigga."

He laughed. "Naw, we got a lot to talk about when all this is settled."

Dear, Vanity 2: Echon's Return   Nona Day

"You married Nika yet?" I asked. He gave me a how you know look.

"Yea, I know how you felt about her as much as you tried to fight it," I said laughing.

"Man, we went through some shit, but we married. Gotta lil daughter on the way," he said proudly.

"Congrats," I said bumping fists with him.

*****

Me and Tree walked into the huge man cave. I remember spending so many nights here going over business or just kicking it with them. Most of the time I was thinking about what it would be like to have Vanity here living a life with me and everyone else. Everyone sat around glaring at me waiting for an explanation.

"Before you put a bullet through my head. Let me state my case. If you feel I'm still responsible for what happened to Bull…do as you must," I said staring at Dose. He was sitting there holding a nine millimeter. His finger was twitching as he held the gun.

"I advise you to speak fast," Fila warned me. Once again, I explained everything to them that I told to Tree. They all sat there speechless.

"We buried your twin?" Fila asked.

"Yea, he was supposed to take over my life in order to gain access and take over the organization. When everything went down with the families, he became too much of me. He died fighting to save Bull's empire," I told them.

"Who shot you?" Dose asked.

"At first I didn't know. I know it couldn't have been any of you. That wouldn't make sense. Now, I know it had to be my uncle. I just don't know why he did all this. He didn't need me to do what he did. He has an entire militia army," I said.

"There's a reason he needed you. We have to find out. Where is he?" Dose asked standing up.

"I don't know. I haven't spoken to him since I arrived here. I'm not sure if he knows Bull is alive or not," I said.

"We taking a trip to Raleigh," Fila said.

"Nah, I'm taking a trip there. The empire he's overseeing is mine. All the men know this. They won't kill me. I need something from you though," I said.

Dear, Vanity 2: Echon's Return   Nona Day

Dose walked over and stood eye to eye with me. "I love you like a brother, but right now all I see is Cain in you. You brought this to Bull's doorstep. Until I have who is responsible for him being in a coma, this is on you."

"Respect," I said.

"What you need?" Tree asked.

"I need for Bull to be pronounced dead," I said. I know they had the power to make it happen. It was obvious their power was even stronger than when I left.

"Why?" Yella Boy asked.

"I need my uncle to think he's dead. I need to know why he needed me to do what he has already done. The only way he will do that is if he thinks Bull is dead," I informed them. Dose and Fila looked at each other.

"How you expect us to trust you?" Dose asked.

Tree cleared his throat. "One word…Vanity."

"I have to see her before I go," I said to Dose.

"You got until tomorrow morning to see her. Tree will be taking the trip with you," he said before walking out the room.

"Damn, you got family. So, what's yo name?" Fila asked.

I chuckled. "My name is Echon. If you need the name to find me if I jump ship, it's Atsu Bello. My uncle's name is Kasim Bello. He resides in Raleigh, North Carolina with a fuckin' harem that's guarded by a militia." They all laughed.

"I don't have much time before morning. Can I go now?" I asked.

"You haven't even asked how Bull is doing," Fila said.

"He's in a coma thinking I betrayed him. I don't need to ask if he's going to make it. I know the nigga ain't leaving Worth," I said.

"You right," Fila said smiling.

"Here take my car. I'll catch a ride with Yella Boy home," Tree said.

"Nah, I just need a ride to my car and where to find her. It's the only thing I have of my father's," I said. He nodded his head.

Vanity

I couldn't believe what was happening. My head was throbbing with so many questions running through my brain. My heart was pounding with so many emotions pumping through my blood. The moment I got back to the hotel I drank everything in the minibar. Nothing would wake me up from when I heard Nika's words. I didn't know if I was having a dream or nightmare. So many nights I prayed for him to be alive. I cried until I couldn't cry anymore. Now that he is alive, I'm not sure if it's a good or bad thing. I was sitting in the middle of the floor rocking side to side trying to wrap my brain around everything when Zelda came rushing inside.

"Vanity are you okay?" She asked rushing over and kneeling on the floor beside me. I heard and saw her kneeling beside me, but I was caught in a trace. I couldn't speak or turn my head to look at her. I was in a state of shock.

"Where's EJ?" I asked staring straight ahead at the crème colored wall. His father is alive. How was I going to explain his father's absence for so many years? Does his return put EJ's life in danger? Was his life in danger? I could feel myself getting overly emotional. My eyes started to tear up.

"He's with Nika and Zuri. I thought it was best he stay with them until you pull yourself together. Vanity, did you drink all this liquor?" She asked.

"Yea, it helped calm my nerves," I said finally turning to look at her.

"Jesus Vanity! You smell like a damn buck barrel. Come on, you need to take a cold shower, so we can talk," she said turning her nose up at me. She tried to help me stand up, but I realized how drunk I was when I fell on top of her.

"Van get yo ass off of me!" She screamed angrily. I don't know why but I started laughing hysterically. I laughed uncontrollably as she tried to push me off of her.

"Bitch, you gone kill me! I can't breathe!" She warned me. In a blink of an eye, my laughter turned into a cry. I finally rolled off of her and onto my back on the floor. I looked up at the beautiful chandelier as tears slid down the side of my face.

"Stop crying Van! Get up! We need to talk!" She demanded stomping her feet. I finally pulled myself off the floor. I could barely walk I was so wasted. She helped me to the bathroom and into the shower. When she turned on the cold shower, I started sobering up.

About thirty minutes later, I walked back into the living area in the complimentary bathrobe. Zelda was sitting on the sofa looking more stressed than I was earlier. I realized how much stress I've bought to her life. She's always pulling me out of some emotional whirlwind. I walked over and sat down beside her.

"I'm sorry Zee. You are supposed to be enjoying your life. Instead you are always trying to keep me sane," I said softly.

She stared at me. "Don't you ever say anything like that Van. I love you like a sister. I will drop everything for you and EJ. I need you as much as you need me. You are my sanity from my own craziness sometimes."

"I love you," I said smiling at her.

"Good, because I'm Echon's lawyer. I went to the precinct to represent him. He's out," she said standing up and walking away from me.

"What?" I asked jumping up in anger. How dare she represent him without speaking with me first?

"I need a drink," she said opening the minibar. It was empty. She looked back at me and rolled her eyes. I shrugged my shoulders.

She grabbed her purse and pulled out a blunt. Zelda always smoked, so it didn't surprise me. She lit the blunt and took two deep hits. I waited until she got over her coughing fit from inhaling too much.

"If I didn't represent him, they would run his prints. We don't know what might come up from his past. I didn't want to take that chance. Another reason was if I didn't find out if he tried to kill Bull, he was going to be a dead man again. I couldn't fathom the thought of you living through his death again," she explained.

"Did he do it?" I asked nervously. She shook her head and it felt as if a ton of bricks were lifted off my shoulders.

"What happened? How is he alive?" I asked.

"I don't know Van. My only concern was saving his life at the time. Fila and Dose were ready to kill. The moment we left the precinct I dropped him and Jedrek off at the hospital. That's why I made sure you wasn't there when he came. I only hope they accepted what he tells them about what happened to Bull. Whatever his story is," she said.

I walked over and flopped down on the sofa. I still had no answers. Nothing seemed real right now. All I wanted right now was to go back to my simple boring life in Atlanta with my son.

"He asked how you were doing. I didn't tell him anything. That's something that should only come from you," she said sitting next to me.

"How is he? Does he act the same? What does he look like? Where has he been?" I rambled my questions.

She snickered. "He's doing well. He still acts a bit special. As for his looks, let's just say you better be glad I'm a loyal bitch. He still looks the same just more muscles. His hair is in small plaits all over his head. His beard his trimmed. It's not as full as it used to be. Don't have a clue where he's been."

I turned my nose up. "He got plaits in his head?" She laughed and nodded her head.

Dear, Vanity 2: Echon's Return   Nona Day

"I don't know when, but he's coming Vanity. You need to mentally and emotionally prepare yourself for it," she warned me.

We jumped when someone banged on my room door. My heart rate skyrocketed. She eased over and tried peeping through the peephole, but she was too short. I was too nervous to move. She asked me with her eyes did I want her to open the door. I took a deep breath and nodded my head. I held my breath until the door opened. I exhaled when I saw Jedrek standing on the other side.

"Come on, let's go," he said to Zelda.

"Nigga, go where?" She asked with an attitude.

"To yo damn room. You don't need to be here with her. That nigga on his way over here," she said glancing at me. My heart and head started pounding.

"First of all, you ain't invited in my damn room. Secondly, I'm not leaving her to deal with this alone," Zelda said bopping her head from side to side. It was time for me to woman up and deal with this situation.

"It's okay, Zee. I'll be okay," I said standing up. She gazed at me seeing the uncertainty in my eyes.

"No Van. I'll stay here with you. I don't know who this fool thinks he is. He's not coming in my damn room," she said glancing at him.

He chuckled and held up a key card. "Don't be too long. I don't have all night." He walked away without giving her a chance to speak. She stood there with her mouth open. I giggled. I don't know much about him, but he was the type she needed to tame her ass.

"Go Zee. I'll be okay," I assured her.

She walked over and sat on the couch. "Well, I'll stay until he comes. Besides, who the hell that fool thinks he is ordering me. I'm fuckin' Zelda Vandross. Luther was my damn cousin." I could always depend on her to make me laugh. She always hollering Luther Vandross was her cousin.

"You are going to carry that lie to your grave," I said flopping on the loveseat across from her.

"Yup," she said proudly.

We sat and talked for over an hour about Echon's return, my relationship with Emmanuel, EJ, and her new friend, Jedrek. Within that hour, I still had no clarity. We were so wrapped up in our conversation we were startled by the soft tap on the door. We sat there staring at the door.

"You've already seen him. Why are you scared?" I asked her still staring at the door.

"I don't know. I guess in some weird way I was thinking maybe this wasn't really happening. Maybe we were imagining all this, but reality is on the other side of the door Van," she said staring just like me.

I took another deep breath and slowly walked over to the door. I looked back at Zelda for support to open the door to my past that I couldn't let go. She nodded her head. I slowly opened the door. There he stood in all his masculine beauty. Heat rushed from the tip of my toes to the top of my head. Goose bumps popped up all over my flesh. Chilling sensations spread through me. My mouth became dry as it fell open. My head started to spin, and my legs became numb. It is him. He is truly alive. Everything started to fade away. I didn't faint, but I couldn't hold myself up any longer. My knees buckled almost causing me to fall. His muscular, tattooed arms caught me before I hit the floor.

Zelda

I jumped off the sofa, so Echon could lay Vanity down. His presence knocked her off her feet. I went to the minibar and grabbed a bottle of water. She chugged the bottle down without stopping. Echon sat across from her on the loveseat just taking all of her in. Even in her worst state Vanity still looked beautiful. I took the empty bottle from her shaking hands. She was a nervous mess. I knew she wasn't okay when her chest started going in and out. She ogled Echon with hate and love in her eyes. He stared back at her with apologetic eyes and love. Her breathing became shallow.

"Van, calm down," I whispered to her. All of a sudden, she jumped up and leaped on top of Echon like a wild cat.

She was clawing and punching him as she screamed out her anger to him. He didn't stop her. He sat there cool as a cucumber taking everything she was giving him. He never raised a hand to stop her. I could feel the pain in her voice. I could also see the hurt in his eyes. This was too damn emotional for me. I wiped the tear that slid down my cheek. I knew I needed to stop her when I saw blood drip from his lip. I moved in to pull her off of him, but he held his hand up to stop me. I stopped in my tracks. He wrapped his arms around her to calm her down. My heart shattered when she let out a cry I hadn't heard from her since Tree told her of his death. She was emotionally exhausted from fighting him. She collapsed on his chest and sobbed softly. I sat there watching him comfort her until I didn't hear her cries anymore. All I heard was light snoring from her.

I stood up. "Don't pressure her to do or say anything she's not ready to discuss. Come get me if she needs me. I'm in penthouse four," He nodded his head. As confused as I am about his return, I know he would take care of her tonight. I left them to try to discuss where they go from here.

I almost had a heart attack when I walked in my room. I completely forgot Jedrek had let himself in. He was in the kitchen cooking. I thought Echon was a little touched. This fool been smothered in crazy sauce. I wanted to be angry about him cooking in the kitchen I had no plans of using, until the aroma of the food hit my nose. I realized I hadn't eaten all day. My stomach started to growl. He placed a plate with a big ass T-bone steak and steak fries on the table. My mouth started to water. I got angry again

Dear, Vanity 2: Echon's Return   Nona Day

when I realized it was only one steak. I know this fool didn't cook in here and didn't think of me.

"You gone stand there looking slow as fuck or sit down and eat?" He asked.

My eyes grew wide. "That's for me?" He just stood there waiting for me to sit down. I sat down at the table as he sat across from me.

"Where's your food?" I asked.

"I ate before I came over. I got that shit out the kitchen," he said nonchalantly.

I snickered. "That's stealing."

He chuckled and shrugged his shoulders. "I'm a criminal. What do you expect?"

I bowed my head to say my grace. Once I was done, I looked up to see him cutting my steak for me. I smiled at him, but he kept a straight face until he was done. I ate a piece of the steak as he watched. I was truly in awe at how tender and juicy the steak was. It was flavored with just the right amount of seasoning. It was a little too pink for me, but I didn't care. It was damn delicious. He poured me a glass of red wine.

Dear, Vanity 2: Echon's Return   Nona Day

"I guess you stole that too?" I asked smiling at him. He shrugged again. I shook my head.

"Why are you doing this for me?" I asked curiously.

"I ain't doing shit for you. I'm doing this for us," he stated bluntly. I gave him a please explain look.

He leaned over and glared into my eyes. "I know shit was crazy today, so you hadn't eaten. I needed to feed you to fuel your body, because I'm going to fuck yo soul from you tonight."

I reached over to slap him, but he caught my hand by my wrist. I stood up struggling to get my arm from him. He stood up and jerked my body into his wide muscular chest. He placed his free hand around my neck.

"So, you gone feed me and rape me?" I asked angrily struggling to get away from him.

"I'm not going to make you fuck me. You are going to fuck me because it's what you want from me. Now, finish eating while I take a shower," he said walking away. I couldn't deny how wet my panties were. *One time. I'll fuck him one time and forget I met his retarded ass. His*

Dear, Vanity 2: Echon's Return   Nona Day

dick probably ain't bout shit anyway. I spoke the words in my head.

Thirty minutes later, my mouth dropped open when I walked in the bedroom. He was standing in all his glorious, dark chocolate, muscular flesh. My mouth watered as my eyes roamed over his body. I gulped down a mouth of saliva when my eyes landed on his massive dick. I'm talking a black Moby dick size. I've fucked some well-endowed men plenty of times, but never this size. It was definitely over ten inches and the thickness was scary. Thick veins ran through his shaft like bolts of lightning. For the first time, I was nervous about having sex.

"Take off your clothes," he demanded staring at me.

"I-I need to shower," I said nervously.

"Nah, if it stank, I'm killing yo ass," he said seriously.

I can't get over how I was letting this fine, rude ass nigga treat me. I need some serious counseling for allowing this. My stupid ass starting undressing as he stood there stroking his beautiful black dick. I nervously stood before him in all my glory. He slipped a condom on as his lust filled eyes roamed over my body.

"Come here," he ordered. I slowly walked over to him. He towered over me as I looked up at him.

He reached around my head and gripped a handful of my long curly extensions. He leaned down and aggressively devoured my mouth with his. His control over me was captivating. I whimpered and moaned as our wet, sloppy tongue kissing generated heat between my thighs. All my inhibitions went away. I wanted to feel this man inside me desperately. He massaged my breasts and pinched my hard nipples as I stroked his throbbing monster. I could feel my wetness between my thighs. He lifted me up wrapping my legs around his waist. I thought he was carrying me to the bed, but my back was pressed against the bedroom wall. He unwrapped my legs from his waist and placed them in the crook of his arms. He started licking, sucking and biting from my neck to my breasts. Every time he tugged on my nipples with his teeth I moaned in pure ecstasy.

"You ready for this dick?" He moaned as he stroked his wet tongue over my breasts.

Dear, Vanity 2: Echon's Return   Nona Day

"Yessss! Pleeaassseee!" I pleaded feeling his mushroom head at my entrance. My pussy was throbbing waiting to feel him inside. He lifted my legs up higher while they were still in his arms. His hands were laying flat on the side of my head against the wall.

When he rammed inside me with no mercy, my scream got stuck in my throat. It felt like he was splitting me apart. I never knew pain could feel so damn good. My mouth fell wide open trying to let out the scream that couldn't escape my throat.

"Sssshhhhit!" He roared buried inside me.

He stood there a few minutes before he started drilling inside me. I wrapped my arms around his back clawing into his flesh. My liquids spilled from me like a running stream. Gushing wet sounds were heard after every thrust. He pulled out leaving the head inside of me, only to ram back inside me sending me spiraling out of control. I cussed, moaned and cried out to our Heavenly Father as I continued to be dickmatized. He drove inside me at an angle hitting a spot that I never felt before. I held on to him for my dear life. I felt like my breath was snatched from my body.

Dear, Vanity 2: Echon's Return   Nona Day

"Aaaaaaahhhh! Yyyyeessss! I'm coooommming!" I screamed as I exploded. My entire body shivered and jerked uncontrollably.

"Yea, that's it. Come all over this dick," he moaned in my ear as he nibbled on my earlobe. He never stopped stroking. I was breathing sporadically.

"Shit, you are a damn creamer," he said looking down at his dick sliding in and out of me.

He carried me over to the bed and placed me on all fours. This was my favorite position, but that orgasm nearly knocked the life out of me. I didn't have much more to give him. I didn't know if I could handle him in this position. He wasn't fully inside me when I was against the wall. This gives him full access. When he rammed his entire thick dick inside me, I tried running from him. He held on to my waist and kept driving inside me as he groaned and grunted.

"Relax this good ass pussy. Stop trying to run," he said slapping my ass.

He dug his fingers into my ass cheeks lifting them to get deeper inside me. I gripped the sheets and screamed his name as another life altering orgasm ripped through me. Again, he didn't stop. I thought he was on the verge of coming. His groans and grunts were getting louder and louder. I didn't know how much more of the unbelievable pleasure my body could take. I could feel him growing inside me. He gripped my hair and pulled me back pressing my back against his chest. He started licking and sucking on my neck as he caressed my breasts.

"You know how got damn good this pussy is?" He whispered in my ear. All I could do was nod. I was experiencing a mini orgasm just from the feel of him inside me.

"Well, fuck me like you know how good it is. Own this mothafuckin' dick."

I don't know why but those words reminded me of who I was. While he was still inside me, I positioned back on all four. I spread my legs and gave my back the ultimate arch. I felt him sliding deeper inside my creaminess.

"Oooh ssshhit! Hell yea! Just like that!" He barked slapping both my ass cheeks.

Dear, Vanity 2: Echon's Return   Nona Day

I started bucking slamming my ass against his pelvis. Slapping and gushing sounds rang out along with our moans and groans. Squeezing his shaft with my walls I twirled my hips. He let out a groan that let me know he was getting ready to cum. I dug my nails into the sheets. I felt myself getting ready to explode with him. He gripped my hips and rammed inside me faster and deeper on every stroke.

"Gooooottt dammmnnn! Aaaarrrggghhh!" He roared as he unloaded inside me. I screamed out in pure bliss as I came with him. Our bodies shivered and jerked until we came down from our sexual high. All of a sudden, he jumped off the bed. He was hopping around on one leg.

"What's wrong?" I asked trying to catch my breath.

"I got a fuckin' cramp," he said trying to put his leg down. I tried not to laugh, but I couldn't hold it. I fell over laughing hysterically. The cramp was still in his leg. He looked like he was in so much pain. I finally stopped laughing.

"Come lay on the bed," I told him. He limped over to the bed with agonizing pain on his face. He laid down and I started massaging the cramp. He breathed a sigh of relief as the cramp went away. I kept massaging as his muscle relaxed. I looked up to see him staring at me. It was a stare I never saw when a man looked at me.

I nervously smiled at him. "What now?"

"I change this rubber and we fuck some more," he said bluntly.

"You sho you able. I mean I don't want you to tap out again," I said feeling confident.

He chuckled. "Exactly how many times did you tap out?" I honestly didn't know. I stopped counting after number three.

"Come on, let's shower," he said getting off the bed.

Echon

I should've been sleeping with her. I hadn't slept since I arrived. I had put her in the bed. All I could hear was her cute little snore. I guess the alcohol I smelled on her breath knocked her out. She's been asleep for more than six hours. She's still as beautiful as the day I left her asleep in my bed. She even smelled the same. I think the only thing about her that has changed is her feelings for me. There was so much anger in her eyes when she stared at me. I touched the cut on my lip that she caused. I felt none of the licks she landed on me. My adrenaline was pumping too fast with all the love I had for her. All I wanted to do was show her how much I missed her. Just as my eyes started to close, she stirred in the bed. She slowly sat up and looked around the room. She hadn't spotted me sitting in the dimly lit bedroom. Her hair was a mess, but it didn't take away from her chocolate beauty. I sat and watched as she climbed out the bed. Still not looking in my direction, she went into the bathroom. I heard the shower come on.

About thirty minutes later, she came out with a towel wrapped around her. I know I had to let her know I was here before she dropped the towel. As tempting as it was to see all of her, I wouldn't disrespect her that way. I cleared my throat making a loud noise as I stood up. She jumped, and screamed being startled by my presence. I stepped into the light, so she could see me.

She stared at me. "I thought I was dreaming."

"It's not a dream Vanity. I'm here," I said walking toward her.

I stood in front of her. She stared up at me. Her hand reached up and caressed the side of my face. I closed my hands and relished in the pleasure of her delicate touch. I wanted to touch her, but I didn't want to ruin this moment.

"How?" She asked wanting to know how I was still alive.

"I will explain everything. Vanity, I really need you to get dressed. We can talk in the living room," I said. I didn't give her a chance to reply. One second later, I would've had my lips on hers.

I was in the kitchen looking for something to cook. She needed some food on her stomach. I know she has to have a hangover. She walked slowly and nervously into the kitchen. She sat at the kitchen isle just staring at me.

"How do you feel?" I asked standing on the opposite side of the isle.

"I feel like I'm in some kind of Twilight zone," she said.

"Let's take a ride. We can put something on your stomach and talk," I told her.

"No, I don't want to eat! I want you to tell me what happened!" She demanded angrily.

I walked around the isle and sat on the stool next to her. There was so much to tell her. She sat and listened to every word up until my arrival back in New Orleans. I could see the disbelief of my story in her eyes. I answered every question she asked.

"So, you have to go and risk your life to save your life?" She asked.

"I have to go and make things right Vanity. If I hadn't returned here, Bull wouldn't be in a coma. He wouldn't be on verge of losing his legacy," I told her.

Dear, Vanity 2: Echon's Return   Nona Day

"What about you? What if you don't return? Then what Echon? I go through the same shit I went through when you left. The same pain I felt when Tree came to visit me?" She asked with worry and anger jumping up off the stool.

"I'll be back Vanity," I tried assuring her.

"You should've never left. You left me in that bed with nothing. Not even a decent fuckin' goodbye. I prayed so many days and nights waiting for you to return."

She walked up to me and eyed me down. "I felt like I couldn't live anymore. It felt like life was draining from my soul. When you first left, I felt like I wanted to die. God blessed me though. He gave me a reason to fight for my life. I don't want you in my life anymore. I don't want to love you anymore. I just want to be free."

She didn't realize she was crying until I reached up and wiped the tear from her cheek. I couldn't help myself. I wanted her to feel how much I loved her. I wanted her to believe I was coming back. I stood up wrapping one arm around her waist. She tried pulling away, but I held her tight. Her eyes met mine and she stop struggling to get away from me. With her mouth slightly opened I leaned down stroking my tongue over her bottom lip. I could feel her body shiver. I could feel my dick growing. She wrapped her arms around my neck pulling my head down to meet her lips. A loud groan came from deep inside me as we indulged in our first kiss in years. It was like nothing had changed. Her mouth was wet, sweet and minty like always. I sat her on the isle, so she could be eye level to me. I broke our kiss to give attention to her neck. I wanted to taste every inch of her body. I broke contact with her long enough to pull her shirt over her head. My mouth started to water as I thought of her taste in my mouth. I pulled my shirt over my head. Her soft hands ran down my stomach as I licked and massaged her breasts.

"I love you Vanity," I moaned in her ear. She started gyrating her hips. She moaned as she felt the friction of my bulge rubbing against her pussy through her shorts. We became like the wild animals I remember when we would fuck each other until we had nothing left to give. She pulled at my jeans until she unbuttoned them. She reached into my boxers wrapping her hand around my shaft.

"Aaaaaahhh Sssshhit!" I groaned loudly at the feel of her delicate hand around my shaft.

Dear, Vanity 2: Echon's Return   Nona Day

I kissed my way down her belly. The banging at her room door caused us to stop immediately. She pushed me out the way and jumped off the isle. I could tell she was mad at herself and embarrassed for letting things get that far between us. No matter what she says. She can't deny what's between us. She pulled her shirt over her head and rushed toward the door. I hurried and put mine on. I didn't want to hear Zelda's mouth about taking advantage of her. I hadn't noticed the sun had come up. I guess we were talking longer than I thought. There was never enough time when I was with her. I walked back into the living room. It wasn't Zelda on the other side of the door when she opened it. It was some nigga.

"Emmanuel what are you doing here?" She asked shocked with her back to me. He barged into the room.

"You called me all upset, asking me to come get you. You was drunk as hell. Talking about your ex was still alive. I was worried about you, so I came," he said glancing at me.

"I did?" She asked surprised. I guess she called him in her drunken state.

Dear, Vanity 2: Echon's Return   Nona Day

She had somebody. It's been years since she saw me and heard of my death. I wanted to be understanding about her moving on with her life, but I couldn't. The thought of another man having her was unbearable. I couldn't help the murderous glare I was giving the dude.

"Who da fuck is this nigga Vanity?" He asked looking at her but pointing at me. I didn't like the way he was speaking to her. She was caught so off guard she didn't know how to reply. I decided to introduce myself.

"I'm Lazarus. The dead boyfriend," I said staring at him. He stood there gazing at me waiting for me to let him know I was just joking. I kept a straight face to let him know I was serious.

"Vanity, what the hell is going on?" He asked giving his attention back to her.

"I'm sorry for making you come all this way Emmanuel. I was just in a state of shock when I found out," she tried explaining.

"You telling me this is your dead ex? Where the fuck is EJ?" He asked angrily. I had no clue who EJ was and didn't care. He had one more time to raise his damn voice at her.

"Echon, I need to speak with Emmanuel alone," she said pleading to me with her eyes. She knew I was seconds away from ending him. That was not the way I wanted to start things off with her again.

"You fucked this nigga?" He roared at her.

That was all I could take. My fist met his throat. He dropped to the floor holding his throat trying to breath. She must've left the door open. Vanity rushed over to help the dude while I stood eye to eye with Quran as he walked in the room. I didn't feel the same brotherly love from him I felt seeing him after so many years. I took it as him being shocked from seeing a dead man. I told him to come with me downstairs to give them time to talk.

Vanity

"It's seven o'clock in the morning. I don't care if the nigga did just come from the dead. What the fuck is he doing here?" Emmanuel asked angrily massaging his throat from the punch Echon gave him. I knew he was pressing his luck by the way he was speaking to me. He always been overprotective of me. I guess that hasn't changed.

I had to lie. He would never understand Echon staying in the room with me last night. "He arrived only thirty minutes before you came."

"What the hell does he want?" He asked.

"I don't know Emmanuel. I'm still in shock he's alive. You almost told him something he knows nothing about," I said in a low voice as if we weren't alone.

"So, he just come from the dead and show up thinking he coming back into your life?" He asked glaring at me.

"I don't know what was in Echon's head about us. All I know is that I have to protect my son."

He walked over and stood in front of me. Emmanuel was only a few inches taller than me, so we were basically eye to eye. "I love you Vanity. I want a life with you and EJ. I hope you are not thinking about letting him back in your life."

I couldn't deny the thought of having Echon in my life again hadn't crossed my mind. I thought of what our life would be like every day. Knowing he was still living a dangerous life complicated our situation even more. I was with Emmanuel now. Emmanuel is a good man that loves me, and his lifestyle doesn't put me and EJ in danger. He's the type of man I need in my life. If only just a simple touch from Echon didn't cause my body to burn like a raging fire.

"I'm with you Emmanuel. You are the one I want a life with, but I can't deny him knowing his son. I have to tell him," I told him.

He flopped down on the sofa and exhaled a deep breath. It was like he was worried I was going to say I wanted to be with Echon, and not him. I feel like such a coward and hypocrite. I was seconds away from feeling what I've longed for since he left. Now, I'm standing here lying to a man that wants to build a life with me. I walked over and sat next to him.

"I'm sorry. I know this is crazy. We'll get through this. I just need time to sort things out with him about EJ," I said omitting that I needed to sort out my feelings for Echon.

"Just promise me you won't let him come between what we are building together," he said looking at me with pity in his eyes.

"He hasn't said he wanted anything with me. You're jumping to conclusions. Let's just take this one day at a time," I said. Lying with the potential of breaking a promise was too much for me. I chose to deflect.

"Him being in EJ's life is not a good idea. You never told me things about him, but I know plenty. He's a criminal. You think EJ needs a father like that in his life," he said.

My blood started to heat up. "You don't know a damn thing about him. He is EJ's father and I will not keep my son from knowing him." I started to walk away. He grabbed my arm and stood up.

"Well, tell me something about him Vanity. You seem to be in your feelings about me speaking on him," he said staring at me.

"I will tell you this. If you attempt to speak to me in a disrespectful tone again, he will kill you. With that being

Dear, Vanity 2: Echon's Return   Nona Day

said, don't speak on someone you know nothing about," I said snatching away from him.

I went to the bedroom. I just needed some time to myself to clear my head. I grabbed my phone and noticed I had a message from Nika. She was letting me know Lamar was coming by with EJ to get his swim trunks. My heart immediately dropped. Echon left the room with Quran, but I didn't know if they were still here. I'm more than sure they were downstairs probably having breakfast. I called Nika, but she didn't answer the phone. I called Quran, but he didn't answer either. I never got Lamar's phone number from her. I couldn't chance Echon running into EJ before I told him. I rushed out the room and to the front door.

"Vanity what's wrong?" Emmanuel asked.

"EJ is on the way here. I have to get Echon out of the hotel. Quran isn't answering his phone," I said frantically before opening the door.

When I opened the door, Zelda was standing there getting ready to knock. I grabbed her by the hand and rushed to the elevator. I told her about EJ being on the way here with Lamar as we went down to the lobby. Quran and Echon was eating breakfast when me and Zelda walked into the dining area. Before I could make up an excuse to get Echon out before they showed up, they came walking into the dining area.

"Uncle Q!" EJ yelled as he ran toward him. I broke out into a cold sweat and my heart pounded.

"He spotted you from behind," Lamar said walking up to us.

"What's up lil man?" Quran said giving him a hug.

"This the best vacation ever! I got everyone here!" EJ said excitedly with the biggest smile on his face.

He started laughing. "Mama where yo shoes?" I looked down and noticed I was barefoot.

Emmanuel walked into the dining area. I had finally let him meet EJ. They got along pretty well. EJ ran over to him and gave him a high-five. Zelda nudged my arm. She nodded her head at Echon when I looked at her. He sat there like a statue staring at EJ with his eyes full of tears. I've seen Echon at his lowest, but never to the point that brought tears to his eyes. I didn't know what to say to him. His eyes stayed fixed on EJ.

Dear, Vanity 2: Echon's Return   Nona Day

"Come on, let's go get your swim trunks," Zelda
said walking over to EJ. She took him by the hand and led
him out the dining area. Echon was stuck. He watched EJ
until he was out of sight. I stood there nervously waiting to
get his attention. He still just sat there speechless.

"Echon," I called his name softly. Still nothing.

He was still as a rock. I walked over and laid my
hand on his shoulder. He finally looked up at me. He
searched my eyes for what he already knew. I gave him
confirmation without speaking a word. He closed his eyes
tightly to fight back the tears. He stood up and walked out
the dining room. I went to follow him, but Emmanuel
grabbed my arm.

"He just found out he has a son Emmanuel. I'm
going to make sure he's okay. We're not the only ones
dealing with his return. This is a lot for him too," I said.

He released my arm and I followed behind Echon
watching him walk out the hotel. When I got outside, he
was standing there looking up at the clear sky. He felt my
presence when I stood beside him.

SOUL Publications

Dear, Vanity 2: Echon's Return   Nona Day

"I was going to tell you. Everything just seemed to be happening so fast," I said softly looking at him.

He turned his head to look at me. "I left you pregnant with our child. I'm sorry Vanity."

"You didn't know," I told him.

"Is that why you hate me?" He asked. It broke my heart to hear him think I hated him. I loved him more than I could ever say in words.

"I don't hate you Echon. I was angry and hurt for a long time when you left. God sent Tree to me to release all of that. I forgave you a long time ago. I understand why you left," I explained.

"If I would've just came to check in on you, I would've known. I thought I was doing the right thing by staying away from you. I fought and prayed every day for strength to let you live a normal life. I left you with more than you should ever go through alone. I can't imagine what you went through," he said. This is why I could never stop loving him. He was so open and genuine with his feelings.

"It was hard, but I had Zee and Quran. I don't blame you Echon. I believe if things hadn't happened to you the way they did, you would've returned eventually," I said.

"That's my son. He looks just like me," he said proudly.

I smiled. "Yes, he does. He has a lot of your ways also. I have pictures of you in his room. I never told him you were dead. It was too much accepting it for myself. I couldn't bare telling him, too."

He placed his hand on the side of my face. Chills ran through my body. "I thought you loving me was my greatest blessing, but you choosing to bear my son when I walked away is a blessing from God. Thank you." My body reacted to him without consent from my mind. I kissed the palm of his hand. He stroked my cheek with his thumb as he stared at me with so much love and admiration. I took a step back when I heard EJ's laughter.

"He laughs like me," he said turning his head to see EJ walking out the Zelda and Lamar. Tree pulled up in front of the hotel. I could tell by the look on his face he was shocked to see EJ here. He jumped out the car and walked up to me.

"He doesn't know yet," I told him.

He looked at Echon. "It wasn't my place to tell you."

Dear, Vanity 2: Echon's Return   Nona Day

"Respect," Echon said nodding his head.

"Are you ready to meet him?" I asked.

He looked at Tree as if he was asking for his approval. Tree stepped away and pulled out his phone. Tree came back giving him a simple head nod. EJ walked over and bumped his fist with Tree. Echon chuckled at EJ trying to act all gangsta. He was still mesmerized by his mini me. EJ finally looked up at him. He studied his face for a few seconds. He looked up at me.

"Mama, he looks like my daddy's picture," he said glancing at Echon. I smiled at him.

I kneeled down to make eye contact with him. "How about skipping the pool and spending the day with me. I have a surprise for you."

"That's what's up. You know the kid love surprises," he said happily. I laughed and shook my head.

Emmanuel and Quran walked out the restaurant. Now, I have to explain to Emmanuel that I'm going to spend the day with my son and his father, the man I couldn't stop loving.

Echon

I told Vanity I was going back to my room to shower and change. She went back upstairs to get dressed with EJ. Emmanuel followed behind her. Tree left to go meet with Fila and Dose about our trip. The plan was to announce his death this morning, but meeting my son changed everything. He came before anything. Zelda was standing there smiling at me.

"What?" I asked.

"I know about the trip you was supposed to take today. You chose her and your son," she said.

"I choose her every time. How the hell you know about the trip?" I asked.

"Yo, bring yo ass back in the room," Drek said walking out the hotel with nothing but his boxers on.

"Oh my God," Zelda said in a low voice. She dropped her head and walked away. I chuckled and shook my head.

I gave Quran a head nod before walking away. We didn't have much time to talk before Vanity and Zelda showed up. I don't know if it was the shock of my return, but I wasn't feeling his vibe. I know I owe him an apology for bolting without a word, but I did what I felt was the best. I know this won't be the last time I see him. I'll sit down and talk with him. Right now, my focus is on my son.

*****

I rushed back to my room to get dressed. I thought my biggest fear was losing her love. Now, it's getting my son's acceptance. I dressed in a pair of black jeans, black tee shirt and black Timbs. I grabbed my jacket and rushed out the door. I was excited and nervous about being introduced to him. When I pulled up to the hotel, I realized I didn't know her phone number. I only had her old one. I still remembered. I'm sure she's gotten a new phone number. I decided to try the number anyway. I was shocked when she answered.

"Hello?" She asked oblivious to the phone number.

"Do you want me to come up?" I asked.

"Oh, I didn't recognize the number. No, we are in the lobby. We'll be right out," she said ending the call.

A few minutes later, they came walking out. I jumped out the car to open the door for them. EJ held up his fist to greet me. I smiled and bumped fist with him. I opened the door and he hopped in the backseat. A breeze caused her scent to travel across my nostrils. My dick jumped just from the scent of her. She was wearing a thin strapped, colorful dress that stopped right below her knees. I don't know how I missed it last night, but I noticed she didn't have her locs anymore.

I touched her hair. "You cut your locs."

"Kinda was a mental breakdown decision," she smiled nervously. The guilt tugged at my heart.

"You are beautiful," I said admiring her. She nervously reached for the door, but I opened it for her.

"Man, this car dope as...," EJ said before Vanity interrupted him.

"Dope as what EJ? Say it, so I can slap the taste out your mouth," she said turning to face him.

"Mama, why you tripping. All I was gone say was the car dope as me," he said shrugging his shoulders. I chuckled.

"Don't entertain his behavior. He hangs around a little kid at school that talks like he's fifteen," she said. I nodded my head.

Dear, Vanity 2: Echon's Return   Nona Day

"I'm new to this. Where are we going?" I asked in a low voice.

"EJ would you like to go to an amusement park or aquarium?" She asked him. He chose both. She informed me he loves looking at all the different fish. I had so much to learn about him.

"How about we hit up the amusement park first. Then the aquarium?" I asked looking at him through the rearview mirror. He smiled and nodded his head. I couldn't get over how much he resembled me.

We rode in silence for a while. "You never changed your phone number."

She looked at me. "You remember the number after all these years. I didn't want to change it in hopes that you might call one day."

She instantly turned her head. "I shouldn't have said that." I wanted to reach over and hold her hand, but I had to remember we weren't alone. As far as he knows, that nigga is her boyfriend.

"Mama, this yo new boyfriend?" He asked nearly knocking the wind from me. She jerked her head around to look at him.

Dear, Vanity 2: Echon's Return   Nona Day

"No, why would you think that?" She asked.

He shrugged. "Because this how I met Mr. Em. Y'all took me to the aquarium and Braves' game."

"I'll explain later. Just be quiet EJ," she said agitated.

"You gotta relax. I'm the one that should be nervous," I told her glancing at her. She laid her head against the headrest and closed her eyes. A few minutes later, she was snoring. EJ sat in the back seat laughing.

"I told her she be snoring," he said laughing. I laughed with him. As I drove, I noticed he kept staring at me.

He unbuckled his seatbelt and leaned forward. "Are you my daddy?" He asked in a whisper. I nearly swerved and hit the car in the next lane. I glanced at Vanity praying she would wake up, but she was out cold.

"You look just like all the pictures Mama shows me," he said.

"Can we wait to talk about this with your Mama?" I asked.

"Ok Daddy," he said sitting back and buckling his seat belt. He looked at me through the rearview mirror smiling. Nothing filled my heart more than to hear him call me Daddy and be happy about it.

The rest of the ride was nothing like I imagined it would be. I thought it would be silent with Vanity's cute snore, but it wasn't. EJ started telling me everything I wanted to know about him. I was elated to know he loved football, but played baseball and basketball also. He asked questions about myself. I answered them as best I could. Meeting my son went nothing like I imagined. It was better. When we got to the amusement park, Vanity woke up. EJ jumped out the car excited about riding the rides and getting a candy apple. We walked toward the entrance like a normal family.

"Damn, I forgot my wallet. I'll catch up," I said.

Vanity smiled at me. "We'll wait here." I jogged back to the car and got my wallet. As I walked back toward them. EJ called me.

"Come on Daddy. I'm ready to ride," he said. Vanity's mouth dropped, and eyes bulged out like a deer caught in headlights.

"He asked me in the car. I told him to wait until you wake up to discuss it. He's a smart kid like his mama," I said to her glancing down at him.

She kneeled down to him. "Are you okay with that? Do you have any questions?"

He smiled. "I'm happy. Now, I get to let my friends meet my Daddy." He glanced up at me. I couldn't help but feel like a proud father.

"Where have you been?" He asked me.

I kneeled down to him. "For a while, I was here in New Orleans while your mother was in Atlanta. She didn't know how to contact me, and I didn't know she had you. If I had known, I would've been here for you and her. I'm sorry. I promise from this day forward to always be here for you."

He wrapped his small arms around my neck. "I'm glad you came back." The joy of him accepting me in his life was overwhelming. I looked up at Vanity as she wiped tears from her cheeks. I held on to my son with a heartwarming hug.

"You gone ride with me Daddy. Mama be scared," he said pulling away from me.

I laughed. "Yea, and we gone make Mama ride."

Dear, Vanity 2: Echon's Return   Nona Day

"EJ what have I told you about speaking proper English?" She said as we started walking again.

The remainder of our day was filled with fun and laughter. I've never been to an amusement park. I think I enjoyed the day more than he did. We could only convince Vanity to go on one ride. That one ride was too much for her. Me and EJ rode every ride at the park. I won him a basketball and Vanity a big teddy bear playing games. After leaving the park, we went to the aquarium. I was amazed at how smart he was. He educated me on so many different fishes as we walked. I thought EJ would be exhausted by the end of the day, but he was still wired.

"Mama, can I go to Uncle Tree's house? We supposed to make smores tonight," he asked as we drove from the aquarium.

"I'll have to call and ask Nika," Vanity said pulling out her phone. She called Nika and chatted for a few minutes. After hanging up, she told me to go to Tree's house.

I chuckled. "I don't have a clue where he stays."

Dear, Vanity 2: Echon's Return   Nona Day

She giggled. "I know something about your friends
that you don't." I laughed. After she told me he bought
Fila's house, I knew where to go.

When we arrived at the house, Nika met us at the
door. She was too anxious to see a dead man still living. I
got a completely different vibe from the Nika I
remembered. She was settled and happy with her life. Her
and Tree still argued like they always did, but the love
between them was real. We sat and talked until EJ and
Baby Gladys begged for smores. We all sat around a
campfire having the best time like two families. I was
determined to get my family back by any means necessary.
EJ and Baby Gladys were knocked out on the sofa when it
was time to go. Nika told us to leave him. I know I was
going out of town tomorrow, so I had to let him know I
would be back. I didn't want him to think I was
disappearing again. I woke him from his sleep to say
goodnight.

"You promise you coming back Daddy?" He asked.
The thought of him thinking I would leave him broke my
heart.

"I promise," I said holding out my fist. He smiled
and bumped my fist before hugging my neck. Vanity gave

Dear, Vanity 2: Echon's Return   Nona Day

him a hug and kiss before we left. The car ride back to the hotel was dead silence. I could see her fuming. I knew exactly why she was mad.

Vanity

I was raging mad. He's returned only to go away again. I'm not stupid. I know where ever or whatever he's going to do is dangerous. I was starting to regret letting EJ meet his father. What if he doesn't return? I would have to break my baby's heart by telling him he's gone. He's so excited about getting a chance to have a relationship with his father. My heart melted seeing them bond. They are so much alike until it's scary. I decided to sit in silence and stew in my anger. I know there was no point in speaking my mind. Echon was going to do whatever he wanted regardless of how I felt, so I kept quiet. On top of that, Emmanuel left going back to Atlanta because he was furious I was spending the day with Echon and EJ. He felt I didn't need to go. I didn't know how EJ was going to react to meeting his dad. If I had known it would go so well, I wouldn't have went with them. I regret I did. Spending the day with him only made me love him more. He's always so caring, gentle and protective of me. There's only one time when he's rough with me. Just thinking of those times caused me to clench my thighs. I was opening the car door before it stopped in front of the hotel.

SOUL Publications

Dear, Vanity 2: Echon's Return   Nona Day

"Woah!" he said grabbing me by the arm.

I jerked my arm from him. "I don't need you to walk me upstairs. You can go. I'm sure you need to rest up for your trip tomorrow." I got out the car before he responded. I couldn't get away from him fast enough. I could hear him calling my name as I entered the elevator. I prayed the doors closed before he caught up with me. My prayers were answered. The doors closed just as he tried to put his arm between them.

When the elevator reached my floor, I hurried off to my room. I was passing the stairway entrance when he opened the door nearly causing my heart to jump from my chest. I was on the eighteenth floor. He wasn't even breathing heavy. We stood there with our eyes fixed on each other not saying a word. I needed to get away from him. I quickly walked away from him. I fumbled around in my purse until I retrieved my key card. My entire body quivered when he wrapped his arm around my waist. He took the key card from me with his free hand and unlocked the door. I tried pulling away from him as I stepped inside the room, but he held on to me.

"Please leave," I said softly as he started kissing on my neck.

Dear, Vanity 2: Echon's Return   Nona Day

I could feel the goose bumps popping up on my flesh. With one hand wrapped around my waist, the other hand slid under my dress. I gasped for breath hearing the thin, lace panties being ripped off of me. He slid his hand between my thighs. I know I should've resisted him. I know in my mind what I was about to do was wrong. I was in a relationship with someone else, but my heart and body reacted to this man in ways my mind couldn't compete with. I quickly pulled away turning around to face him. I stood there watching him pull his shirt over his head. I bit my bottom lip as I ogled his washboard abs. Whatever restraint I was holding on to went flying out the window, along with all the guilt I was feeling for being unfaithful to Emmanuel.

My body and heart wanted this man more than I ever had. I pushed him against the door attacking his mouth and neck like a sex crazed whore. I moaned into his mouth as we indulged in a deep, wet, passionate kiss. I licked, sucked, and bit his neck as he tore my straps from my dress causing it to fall to the floor. I started unfastening his jeans as I kissed my way down his chest to the V-shape that leads to the place that would give me a heavenly high. I pulled his boxers down with his jeans. His rock hard rod leaped out like it was ready for takeoff. When I stroked my tongue over the head, a loud grunt came from him as his dick jumped hitting the tip of my nose. I wrapped my hand around his muscular shaft and he slammed the back of his head against the door. Everything he taught me about pleasuring him replayed in my head. My tongue started licking up, down and all around until he couldn't hold his groans. Both my hands massaged his shaft, I licked and sucked his dome before sliding him all the way in my mouth. I lapped my tongue over his dome to savor the taste from his precum. I started sucking and slurping him in and out as saliva drenched my mouth. I could feel him pulsating in my mouth only making me want more. I wanted to taste every drop from him. I reached down massaging his nut sack as I continued to enjoy having him in my mouth. Saliva drooled down my chin and spilled down to his balls as I massaged them. I could hear him murmur my name, but I couldn't stop. Everything I was doing to him was causing wetness to slide down my inner thighs. I moaned up and down him as I intensified my strokes. His hands gripped a handful of my hair pulling me up off the floor. He slammed his tongue into my mouth as he started ripping my clothes off of me. My body was so overheated to have him I became dizzy. I can't even remember how we ended up in the bedroom. He laid me across the bed pushing my legs in the air and spreading them so far apart my pelvis

ached. He dove into my soaked womanhood like a barbaric

animal growling and grunting as he licked, slurped and

sucked me. I couldn't control the moans and screams that

came from me as he saturated his face with my wetness.

My juices seeped down between my butt cheeks only to be

sopped up by his tongue. My body quivered uncontrollably

from the sensations that ran through my spine. His sharp

tongue darted in and out of my tunnel as his tongue

caressed my swollen bud. I grabbed two handfuls of his

hair as I felt a cosmic orgasm building. I tried pushing his

head away because it felt like my heart was going to

explode along with my womanhood. He pressed his tongue

against my throbbing bud sending me to a world filled with

exploding, colorful, bright stars.

"Aaaaaaahhhhh! Eeeeecccchhhoooonnn!" I cried

out clinching his head between my thighs. Tears flowed

down the side of my face as my body quaked and jerked.

He wrapped his arms around my thighs pulling them apart.

He continued to devour me until my soul was staring down

at my naked body. All I could muster out was soft

whimpers. I was in full tears as orgasms where shooting

through my body from slight touches of his tongue. He finally stood up and stared down at me.

His face glistened from my wetness and my essence dripped from his neatly trimmed beard. He wrapped his hands around my ankles and licked and sucked each one of my toes as he stared into my low eyes. Placing my legs on his shoulders he laid his body on top of mine. We lay there staring at each other with so much love and hunger for each other with his head at my dripping entrance. His lips brushed against me. I bit on his bottom lip before sucking it into my mouth. He pressed his knees into the bed and hunched over me pushing my knees on the sides of my head. Moans and groans of euphoria came from us as he drove inside of me. I could live a thousand lives, and no one could give me the feelings he does. His rod was being smothered with my wet walls. I gripped the sheets as he started slamming inside me the way I loved.

"Sssshhhit!" He groaned as he rammed in and out. He was hitting every wall, corner and angle inside me. I could feel that fire inside of me that I had longed to feel for too long. Again my body reacted to every thrust he gave me. I thought I had nothing else to give, but he proved me wrong. My essence squirted like a fire hydrant when he

Dear, Vanity 2: Echon's Return   Nona Day

slammed into my soft spot. He pulled out of me to lick and slurp every drop as I came. He slid back inside me licked my lips and slipped his tongue in my mouth for me to taste my own flavor. He started back drilling inside me. Every time I would cum, he would head dive between my thighs. I felt like I was in some kind of seventh heaven. My body was experiencing a supernatural high. He gazed into my eyes as he was pounding in and out of me.

"I'm fuckin' home Vanity," he said grunting between each word as he thrust inside me. I felt his rod growing and pressing against my slippery walls. A scowl covered his face as his abdomen tightened.

"Unh Unh!" He grunted like a caveman as he hammered inside me until I felt myself getting ready to release with him.

"Oooohhh Yeeesss! Go deeper, please!" I screamed as bolts of electricity traveled from my toes to my heart. He did just like I begged. It felt like the tip of his rod was stroking my heart causing shock waves in it.

"Echon," I pleaded with a low voice. He slammed inside me in an angle hitting my spot he knows would cause me to lose all sense of reality. I became a wild woman with his beastly strokes. We matched stroke for stroke until our sweaty bodies exploded together.

"Aaarrrggghhh! Ssshhhiiiit! Aaaarrrgghhh!" He roared angrily as he released inside me as I sprayed him with my essence. His body convulsed and mine quivered. Echon wasn't done with me. He was still hard inside me. He flipped me over laying me flat on my stomach. He lay on top of me sliding back inside me and started again. I was emotionally, physically and mentally drained by the time he was done with me. The same way I couldn't remember how I ended up in the bedroom, I couldn't remember how I ended up wrapped in his arms in the tub. My head was laying against his chest when I came back to reality. The hot water was soothing against the soreness between my thighs. He bathed me and carried me to the bedroom. I have no idea when he changed the sheets, but the bed was perfectly made. He laid me in the bed and slid in next to me.

The next morning I woke up, my heart shattered in a thousand pieces. It felt like déjà vu. I awakened to an empty bed. I slowly pulled my emotionally and sexually drained body from the bed. I walked slowly from the bedroom as I felt the soreness from our night of unsurmountable bliss. I washed my face and brushed my teeth before walking into the living room. I was too drained to even put on clothes. I smiled and bit my bottom lip as he sat on the couch with a tray full of food from room service. His back was facing me, so I sneaked up behind him. At least I thought I was until he pulled me over his shoulder and on to the couch. I laughed being caught off guard by his quickness.

"I can smell your presence a mile away," he said looking at me. I smiled and sat up.

"Eat," he said taking the lids off the plates. The French toast, spinach, mushroom and cheese omelet, and potatoes looked scrumptious. He didn't have to tell me twice. I was famished. He stopped me before I started eating by holding my hand. A big grin spread across my face when he bowed his head to pray. I bowed my head and listened as he prayed for God's guidance, strength, mercy and protection for us. I smiled when he cut into his nearly burnt steak.

"EJ likes his meat cooked exactly like you. He won't eat his bacon unless it's almost burnt to a crisp," I said.

Dear, Vanity 2: Echon's Return   Nona Day

"Smart young man," he said glancing at me. I giggled.

We sat and ate breakfast talking about his life the last year. He told me things he learned about his father and mother. I told him stories about EJ. There was two big pink elephants in the room that neither of us wanted to discuss. One was whether he was leaving or not. The other was Emmanuel. He looked at his phone when a text came through. I saw the look in his eyes. I knew he was getting ready to leave. He looked at me.

"I'll be back Vanity," he said.

I stood up and looked down at him with anger and hurt. "Don't bother. We won't be here waiting for you like a damn fool again."

I stormed in the bedroom and slammed the door. I grabbed some yoga shorts and tank top to put on. I needed to talk to Zelda. I realized I hadn't seen her since yesterday morning. I immediately started to worry because she hasn't called or texted. Echon walked into the bedroom standing in front of me. He kissed my lips softly.

"Rather you here or Atlanta. I'm coming back for my family. It would be wise for you to get shit straight with yo lil boyfriend. I love you Vanity," he said before walking out the room.

Zelda

I don't know if I'm being held against my will or not. He took my phone, took the room phone to the front desk, and wouldn't let me leave the room. He insisted I walk around in nothing but my flesh. For the past twenty-four hours I have been fucked in positions I didn't think was possible. My body came in ways unimaginable. The way his dick worked me had me questioning my sanity. I didn't know if I ever wanted to leave this room. I sat at the kitchen isle staring at him as he prepared us breakfast. He was the rudest, most disrespectful, arrogant, thoughtful thug ass gentleman I ever met. No, I've never met a man even close to being like him. Most men are either an asshole, whimps or a gentlemen. He was a mixture of them all. He would say something rude and disrespectful only to do something nice to me. He shampooed my hair and greased my scalp after it dried. He bathed me and oiled my body down as he licked every inch of my flesh. The only thing he hasn't done was eat me out. I was starting to wonder why. I don't give a damn how good his dick is, I need my coochie ate out occasionally. I'm lying. This fool's dick was enough to compensate for anything.

Dear, Vanity 2: Echon's Return   Nona Day

"You don't eat pussy?" I asked him with his back to me as he scrambled eggs. He glanced over his shoulder at me but didn't reply.

"I need my phone. I need to call Van," I told him.

"She's with her nigga. Eat," he said sitting a plate in front of me. This fool could really cook. I'm glad because my ass couldn't cook shit. I was shocked to hear Vanity was with Emmanuel. I just know after spending the day with Echon and EJ she would end up breaking things off with Emmanuel. I started to worry how things went with Echon and EJ. They couldn't have went well if she's still with Emmanuel.

"I still need to check on her. She's probably blowing up my phone," I said.

"What you need to do is eat this food, so we can fuck," he said bluntly. He didn't stop. My mind didn't know how much more I could take but my body reacted to the thought of getting more of him.

"We have done nothing but fuck since you welcomed yourself in my room. I need a break," I said.

He leaned over the isle and glared at me. "Blame yo pussy, not my dick. I'm going to fuck you until my dick stops getting hard when I think about yo pussy. Then and only then will I free you." *What the fuck?* This fool has made me his sex slave and my dumb ass pussy jumped at the thought of it.

"Besides she hasn't called or texted you," he said turning back to the stove.

My eyes grew wide. "How do you know?" I know he wasn't going through my phone.

"I jail broke yo phone while you were sleep," he said nonchalantly. All my blood rushed to my head. Before I knew what I was doing, the plate of food he prepared for me hit him in the back. I jumped of the stool and charged him.

"Nigga, who do you think you are! Gimme my got damn phone!" I screamed trying to land a punch. He wrapped his arms around me and sat me on the isle. He stared licking and sucking on my neck and down to my breasts.

"Put my dick in this good ass pussy," he demanded scooting me to the edge of the isle. My dick whipped ass forgot all about him breaking into my phone. I pulled the one eyed monster from his boxers. He rammed into me with no remorse. He fucked me relentlessly until my creaminess dripped from the counter to the floor. I jumped when someone knocked on the door. He was still hard after coming. When he pulled out me, I realized he had a condom on. I'm glad he was being responsible because I wasn't thinking with a clear head.

"When you stop letting other niggas stick they dick in you, I'll eat yo pussy. Now, go put on some clothes," he said pulling the condom off, threw it in the trash and stuffing his dick back in his boxers. Did he just ask me to be his girlfriend? Or is his jealousy just showing? He lifted me off the counter and walked away. I walked to the bedroom as he slipped on a pair of jeans that laid over the couch.

When I came back into the living area, Vanity was sitting on the sofa while Jedrek cleaned up the kitchen. She gave me a puzzled look. Vanity had a glow in her eyes that I hadn't seen in years, but her face seemed stressed. I gave her a hug and sat down on the love seat across from her. She glanced back at Jedrek and giggled.

"Damn, you got him cooking?" She asked.

"Girl, he fuckin' retarded or something. I've been kidnapped to be his sex slave I think," I whispered glancing at him. She burst out laughing quickly covering her mouth.

She fell over on the sofa trying to muffle her laugh. He walked over and tossed my phone to me.

"It's not kidnapping when you love being fucked into another world. I'm gone take a shower and get out y'all way for a little while," he said walking away. Vanity sat up. We watched him walk into the bedroom with our mouths' open.

"Don't ever call Echon special again," she said smiling.

I giggled and shook my head. "Speaking of slowness. How did it go yesterday?" She rolled her eyes at me.

She started from the beginning telling me about their family outing. I was elated to know EJ was excited about meeting his dad. Just as she was getting ready to tell me the juicy stuff, Jedrek walked back into the living area. He walked over to me, leaned down and gave me a slow, deep, passionate, long kiss that left me dizzy.

"You can leave the room, just make sure to return with that good pussy," he said against my lips with my mouth slightly open. He nodded at Vanity and walked out the room.

"Damn, that was hot," she said staring at me.

"Bitch, why you think I haven't tried to escape. I've been in the room naked for the past day getting my back broke. He had me hanging off the balcony fucking me from behind. I was howling at the full moon like a damn wolf," I said. She laughed.

"He wouldn't let you leave the room?" She asked.

"At first, but then I think I developed Stockholm Syndrome," I said shrugging my shoulders. She couldn't stop laughing.

"We'll talk about him later. I need to know how you ended up with Emmanuel and how he put that glow in your eyes," I said.

She gave me a confused look. "I wasn't with Emmanuel last night."

"Oh shit! I assumed Jedrek was talking about him when he said you was with yo nigga," I said laughing. She went on to tell me how she ended up with Echon in her room. She told me about him leaving this morning. It explained the glow in her eyes and stress on her face.

"He'll be back Van. He's doing what he has to do," I tried assuring him.

"I'm just so confused Zee. I want him in EJ's life, but I don't want the dangerous life he lives. It's damn scary how much I still love him. I don't think it's normal to love someone this much. On top of that, look what I'm doing to Emmanuel. I can't break his heart like this. He doesn't deserve this," she said.

"Echon would never put you or EJ's life in any danger. We can't help who we love Van. I have nothing against Emmanuel, but I know who your heart belongs to. It would be cruel to him to try and make yourself love him when it's impossible," I said.

"I would jeopardize every day of my life to be with Echon, but not my son. I will not let him live that kind of life. I'll walk away from Echon before that happens," she stated adamantly. It was no question in my mind she would.

"Whatever you choose to do, I'm here for you. Regardless, I think you should end things with Emmanuel. You'll never be able to love him as long as Echon is living," I advised her. She nodded her head.

"I'll talk to him when we get back home," she said softly.

She smiled. "You should see them together Van. Echon acts more like the child than EJ. They had so much fun together yesterday."

"And you worried about someone getting in the way of him bonding with his son and having you back in his

life. Trust me, it's not going to happen," I said smiling at
her.

She smiled nervously. "I hope so."

"Anyway, what's on the agenda for the day? I'm
tired of being cooped up in this room," I asked standing up.

"I wanted to visit Worth. Then, we can enjoy the
city. Nika invited us over for dinner later. EJ is hanging
with Fila and his son today," I said.

"Hell yea, I remember you said she can cook her ass
off."

"I'm going to get dressed. I'll be back in a hour,"
she said walking to the door.

Later That Day

Me and Vanity went to visit Bull and Worth. It was
like trying to get into the White House. They wasn't
playing about his security. We were shocked to see he was
awake. He was still hooked to a lot of machines and barely
conscious, but he was alert. Worth looked better than she
did the day we saw her. We only stayed a little while to
show our support. Worth was humbly grateful for our visit.
We did a lot of shopping. I don't know what it was, but I
felt like someone was following and watching us. I didn't
say anything to Vanity. I didn't want her to freak out

thinking our lives were in danger. I was relieved when we finally left the mall. Something felt off, I just wasn't sure what it was. We went back to our rooms to drop our bags off. I was startled when I turned on the bedroom light. Jedrek was laying in the bed on his back. He opened his eyes when I turned on the light.

I dropped my bags and walked over and straddled his lap. It was downright sinful the way I craved him. It surprised me when he sat up and moved me from his lap. I sat with my back pressed against the headboard like him. I gave him a look wanting an explanation for moving me.

"Tell me about yourself," he said. I was shocked by his statement. Most men pretended to want to know about you to have sex with you. I've never had one that took an interest in me after we had sex. Maybe that's because I made it clear I wasn't looking for nothing more than great sex with them.

"Not much to tell," I said shrugging my head.

He gave me a look that told me to do as he said. I started telling him all about Zelda Vandross. I was an only child to a successful lawyer for a mother and successful stock broker and investor father. I was spoiled but my parents instilled hard work, humility, family and loyalty in me every day. I didn't ask them for much. Occasionally, I would remind them they were the ones that spoiled me by going on lavish vacations at their expense. Vanity was the sister I never had. I always felt like the big sister even though she was older. He sat and listened as I told him things about me, I've only shared with Vanity. After I was done, he reached on the nightstand for a bag.

"Here's a new phone. It's the latest iPhone." He placed the bag in my lap and got off the bed. I was so eager to have some of him. I didn't notice the overnight bag sitting by the bedroom door. He walked toward the door. I jumped off the bed.

"Where are you going?" I asked.

"Back to Atlanta. It's been fun," he said winking at me. He leaned down and kissed me softly. I know this nigga ain't just dismiss me like I was nothing, but he did. He walked out the room with his bag. I might have let him control me sexually, but I will not run behind him. As bad as I wanted to run after him and beg for more of what I know I'll never experience again, I stood still. *Fuck him!* I thought to myself. Too bad that's exactly what I wanted to do.

Echon

I felt like I was floating on a cloud as I drove back to Raleigh. I could still taste her on the tip of my tongue. The love we had for each other couldn't be denied. I understand her being scared, but I didn't like her doubting me. My only goal on this earth is to be a family with her and our son. I will destroy anyone or anything that stands in my way including my uncle. I enjoyed the ride with Tree. It gave me a chance to reconnect with him. I was proud of his growth. I never thought I'd hear myself say Nika was good for him, but she was. He's nervous and excited about becoming a father. There's no doubt in my mind he'll be a great one.

"Damn, I thought you was living in hell. This house is about big as Bull's," he said as we drove up the long driveway.

I chuckled. "It was hell in my mind."

I was shocked to see there was no security. The place looked deserted. I used my key Kasim gave to let myself in. The place was so huge we had to separate to see if we could find anyone. Minutes later, we met in the living room on the bottom floor. Neither of us had found a living soul in the house. Tree followed me to Kasim's library. Me and Tree stared down at his lifeless body with his brains splattered on the floor. I was here to rage war with my uncle. I guess he wasn't trying to betray me. My only guess is Thomas betrayed him.

"Damn," Tree said glancing at me.

"I need to find Thomas," I said walking out the room.

"I'll get a cleanup crew here for your uncle," Tree said following behind me. I didn't want his body burnt to ashes. I know he sent me on a mission to destroy Bull, but I feel he thought he was getting vengeance for my parents. I will give him a proper burial next to them.

"Don't burn his body. I want to bury him. He didn't betray me. Thomas betrayed him," I explained to Tree. He nodded his head.

I needed to get back to New Orleans. My focus now is on killing him and protecting my family before he harms anyone else. He had to have taken control of the army that guarded the house. It made me wonder if any of them were now in New Orleans. We didn't waste any time gassing up and driving back home. Tree called Dose and Fila to give them an update. They told us to meet them at the hospital.

My first concern was making sure Vanity, EJ and Zelda were safe. I told Fila to have men guard them from a distance. I know if Vanity knew she was being guarded she would freak out.

New Orleans

Dose and Fila were sitting in the waiting area when we arrived. Sheba and Worth were in the room with Bull. We sat down to discuss the next move. The first thing we needed to do was find Thomas. I gave them the little information I had on him. I know all Genius needed was his phone number to track him down. I didn't even have his phone number. All I had was his name.

"Everyone is at your house. It's being watched. I would advise y'all to tell them to be careful of their movements until we find him. Paisley's there too. She knows, but I told her not to tell them they have security on them," Fila said looking at Tree. Me and Tree nodded our heads.

"I need to speak to Bull," I said. Dose pulled out his phone and called Sheba. A few minutes later, she came out the room smiling.

Dear, Vanity 2: Echon's Return   Nona Day

"He's doing so much better. He's trying to make them release him," she said happily. It took a lot of weight off my shoulders to know he was doing much better.

"Stubborn as a bull," Dose said smiling and shaking his head.

When I walked in the room, Worth had the biggest smile on her face. She stood up and hugged my neck. "Thank you for saving his life," she whispered in my ear. I still felt somewhat responsible for him being here.

"I'll leave you two to talk," Worth said.

"No, I know he hides nothing from you. You don't have to leave. I'm only here to apologize for bringing harm to your doorstep," I said to her. Bull cleared his throat to get my attention. He had a notepad and pen laying on his lap. He couldn't speak with the tube in his mouth. He started writing.

No apology needed
Brothers always

I sat down and explained to him how I'm still alive and how I ended up at his house that night. After I explained everything to him up to this moment he started writing again.

I knew nothing about your parents. Speak with Chiraq.
He's the only one remaining of the original families that
would know

I nodded my head at him. He smiled even though the tube
was in his mouth.

Glad to have you home, Brother

"Good to be home fam," I said smiling back at him.
He raised his arm, and we gave each other a brotherly
handshake. I stayed a while and chatted with Bull and
Worth. I was ready to see my family. I told Dose and Fila
to contact me as soon as possible if Genius comes up with
anything. Me and Tree headed over to his house. Fila
followed behind us in his car.

*****

When we got to the house, everyone was in the
backyard. Paisley was on the grill being the tomboy she
always have been. Vanity, Nika and Zelda were in the pool
with the kids. She looked at me and a big smile full of love
spread across her face.

Dear, Vanity 2: Echon's Return   Nona Day

"Daddy!" EJ yelped swimming toward the edge of the pool. I helped him get out giving him a tight hug. I didn't care about getting my clothes soaked.

"Who taught you how to swim?" I asked putting him down.

"Uncle Tree. I know how to backstroke, swim underwater and dog paddle," he said proudly.

"I looked at Tree and thanked him with a head nod. Even though I was grateful for what he did, I hated I've missed out on so much of his life.

"Daddy will you throw the football to me. Them girls don't know how. Paisley do, but she cooking for us," he said.

"How about you and Fiji throw it to me? Let's see your quarterback skills," I told him as I watched Vanity dry off.

"Yaaayy!" He yelled running over to get his football.

Vanity walked passed me and into the house. I followed behind her into the kitchen. She was leaning against the kitchen isle with her arms crossed when I

Dear, Vanity 2: Echon's Return   Nona Day

walked in. Even when she's upset with me, her love still shows in her eyes.

"Still twisting your hair I see," she said. I hadn't realized I was twisting it. I chuckled. I walked up and placed my hands on each side of the counter locking her in. I gently pressed my lips against hers. She unwrapped her arms holding my face between her hands.

"I missed you," she said against my lips before sliding her tongue in my mouth.
"We going to Jamaica tomorrow," I said after breaking our kiss.

"What?" She asked happily shocked. I didn't have plans of taking them with me, but I felt like they would be safer with me. Besides, I didn't want to infuriate her by leaving again.
"Yea, me, you and EJ. I'm sure Zelda is going to invite herself," I said smiling. She giggled because she knows it was the truth.

"I love you," she said softly. I completely forgot where we were. I kissed her passionately and sat her on the counter pushing her bikini bottoms to the side. I guess she was lost in the moment also as she released my hard dick from my jeans. Just as I was about to slide into her, she stopped me.

"Someone might walk in. And we can't on their counter," she said shamefully.

I looked around the kitchen and spotted the pantry door. I smiled, lifted her up and carried her inside. I pinned her against the door before burying myself deep inside her. My knees buckled at the feel of her wet, warm walls gripping my dick. I gave her slow, deep strokes as we stared at each other. Her sweet juices coated my dick and slid down to my cum filled balls. Her fingertips traced my lips as we glared at each other with passionate and lust filled eyes.

"I want to feel you come inside me," she said desperately. She wrapped her arms around my neck burying my face into the crook of her neck. I placed her legs in my arms and put a hump in my back. I started drilling deeper, harder and faster inside her. I know our moans and groans could be heard on the other side of the door.

Dear, Vanity 2: Echon's Return   Nona Day

"Oooohh Gggggod! I'm 'bout to cuuumm!" She murmured as I was winding my pelvis hitting every spot inside her I knew would send her over the edge. All I could do was grunt to let her know I was almost there. A few more pumps and we were exploding together as our bodies quivered and jerked.

A few minutes later, we walked back out on the deck. Nika looked at us with her nose turned up. "I left washcloths and towels in the spare room that EJ sleeps in when he's here." Vanity giggled and covered her face from embarrassment.

"Out here being a whole freak in my pantry. Vanity I'm shocked, but proud to call you my friend," Nika said laughing. Vanity rushed back inside. All the adults laughed. I was glad the kids were in the yard.

"I'm taking the trip to Jamaica with you," Tree said.

I nodded my head. "I'm taking Vanity and EJ."

"So, y'all just gone leave me?" Zelda asked with an attitude.

"Zelda, I don't have to invite you. That's written in stone that you go where ever Vanity goes," I said winking at her. She smiled.

SOUL Publications

"Well, if they going. Me and Baby Gladys going," Nika said with an attitude. Tree looked at me and I shrugged my shoulders. It didn't matter to me who went. I was just going to get some answers to stop Thomas.

"Y'all make me damn sick. I can't go, because I gotta hair show to attend," Paisley said pouting. We laughed.

I went upstairs to join Vanity in the shower. Zelda stopped me before I started walking up the stairs.

"It felt like someone was following us yesterday. Vanity didn't notice it, but I felt it. I might have been just paranoid," she said. I didn't get security on them until a few hours ago, so it couldn't have been them.

"My uncle is dead. I think his son, Thomas did it. He's the one shot Bull. I have security following y'all every move now. I'm not sure if he is following you. Just be careful how you move," I warned her.

"Is this why we going to Jamaica?" She asked me.

"That and to enjoy some time with Vanity and EJ," I said.

She smiled. "I'm glad you're back. Even though she's stressed, she has that glow in her eyes again."

"Thanks Zee," I said winking at her.

Dear, Vanity 2: Echon's Return   Nona Day

"But don't tell her the reason we going," she warned me. I nodded my head before heading upstairs.

Vanity

We enjoyed the rest of our evening at Nika and Tree's house. I noticed Zelda wasn't her usual self. I made a mental note to go to her room when we get back to the hotel to talk to her. We all rode back in Echon's car. I told Echon to stay in my room with EJ until I go talk to Zelda. I couldn't let him stay the night in my room with EJ there. As far as EJ knows, Emmanuel is my boyfriend and Echon is only his father. We have a lot of explaining to do to him. I knocked on Zelda's door and she let me in with a confused look.

"What's wrong?" She asked.

"Nothing is wrong with me. I came to find out what's wrong with you. You've been acting distant since we got to Nika's house," I said flopping on the sofa.

She chugged from the bottle of wine she was drinking. "He's gone. Nigga came here and fucked me until I couldn't walk straight and just left. No excuse or explanation. Just left."

SOUL Publications

Dear, Vanity 2: Echon's Return   Nona Day

"Where did he go?" I asked. She informed me he went back to Atlanta before taking another swig from the bottle.

I relaxed. "Well, I'm sure you'll see him when we get back home."

"No, I won't. Not once did he say I'll see you when you get back. I'm damn sho not going to go look for him. I have too much pride," she said.

"Well, if you don't care why are you sulking in a bottle of wine?" I asked. Zelda has always been the one in control with any man she's with. Even with some of the psycho type street boys, she called the shots. I don't think she was in control with this one. This was new to her.

"I don't know," she said finishing off the bottle. She's going to have a massive headache in the morning. She walked away and came back with a small bottle from the mini fridge.

"Here, drink with me," she said passing me a small bottle of Hennessy.

"You know I can't handle brown," I reminded her. She passed me a bottle of vodka. She chugged down the Hennessy while I sipped on the vodka. I had to keep a clear head. EJ was in my room tonight.

"Do you like him?" I asked.

"I can't like someone I know nothing about. All we did was fuck. He fucked me so damn beautifully until I wanted to know things about him outside of the bedroom," she said.

"When we get back why don't you try getting to know him?" I asked.

"Because Van, he's a criminal. You know how I feel about dealing with men like that now. I've watched too many women cry over men getting sent to prison. They're left to take care of kids they can't afford anymore. Then the women find out the man has two or three other children on the outside along with all the side bitches. All of them sitting in the courtroom together. Nope, that won't be me."

I couldn't help but laugh. "Now who's being dramatic."

"I'm serious Van. I see it almost every day," she said seriously.

"First of all, you can take care of yourself. You would never just live off what a man has. Secondly, you have to take a chance Zee. I see how you've been changing your heart and mind on love. You want it, but scared to put yourself out there for it," I told her.

Dear, Vanity 2: Echon's Return   Nona Day

"I thought I was just going through some kind of mental breakdown about wanting love and a family, but I want it Van. I want to love someone enough to build a family with him," she said.

"Well, let your guard down. See if he's the one that you can love," I advised her.

"I'll think about it," she said rolling her eyes at me. I laughed and shook my head.

"Thanks for coming to check on me," she said smiling.

"You always my shoulder to cry on. Don't ever think you can't cry on mine Zee," I assured her.

"Okay, remember you said that when I fall in love and sitting in the courtroom surrounded by two baby mamas and three side bitches," she said laughing. I laughed with her. We sat and chatted before I returned to my room.

When I walked in my room, I couldn't help but smile. Echon and EJ were both stretched out on the sofa asleep. EJ had on pajamas. Echon must've made sure he took a bath. He was dirty from playing outside all day. I didn't want to wake them, so I left them there. I went to my bathroom and took another shower. I slipped on a night gown and climbed in my bed. I was in a deep sleep when I felt his arm wrap around my waist.

"I put him in his bed. Do you want me to leave?" He whispered in my ear as he nibbled on my lobe.

I turned to face him. "No, I don't ever want you to leave again."

"I'll leave out before morning, so he doesn't see me in here. I'll crash on the sofa," he said. I nodded my head. He rolled on his back and I rested my head on his broad chest. It didn't take long before both of us were fast asleep.

Next Morning

"Will you two please stop, so I can pack EJ's things," I said to EJ and Echon. They were having a pillow fight in EJ's bedroom while I was trying to pack his things for our trip. Echon acted more like the child than EJ when they were together.

"Okay, we are going to get out your way. We going down to get some breakfast," Echon said.

"Mama, I'll bring you something back. Me and Daddy getting steak, eggs and potatoes. That's a man's meal. We'll get you something for a girl," EJ said. Me and Echon laughed.

"Well, thank you. Bring me an omelet, sausage and toast," I said looking down at EJ.

"Come on Daddy. Let's go," he said rushing out the room.

Echon walked over and placed his hand on the side of my face. He leaned in giving me a sweet, sensual kiss but I'm always greedy. I sucked his tongue in my mouth turning it into a heated, passionate one. We broke our kiss before EJ came rushing back in the room.

"Daddy, come on," he said impatiently. I giggled as my two men left the room.

After packing EJ's things, I went to my bedroom to pack mine. I looked at my phone to see if I missed any calls. I had several from Emmanuel. My heart ached at what I was going to do to him. If Echon hadn't returned I would've chose to build a life with Emmanuel. But Echon's return changed that. I couldn't fight what my heart felt for him. I sat down on the side of the bed and dialed his phone number. He answered on the second ring.

"Hi," I said softly.

Dear, Vanity 2: Echon's Return   Nona Day

"Vanity, I'm sorry for the way I've acted. I'm just so scared of losing you. I love you. I know we can have a great life together. I know you have things to sort out with EJ's father. I will try to be understanding and supportive," he ranting emotionally.

I just couldn't bring myself to say it. At least I owed it to him to say what needs to be said in person. "We will talk when I get back. Thank you for trying to understand."

"I'll be here when you return," he said.

"Okay, have a good day Emmanuel," I said before ending the call. I felt like the lowest person on earth.

About an hour later, Echon returned back to the room. I was sitting on the sofa scrolling through my phone looking at fun things to do with a child in Jamaica. I've been before with Zelda. The fun we had wasn't for children.

"Where's EJ?" I asked.

"Downstairs with Zelda. What's bothering you?" he asked as he sat next me.

Dear, Vanity 2: Echon's Return   Nona Day

"Emmanuel called. I feel awful for what I'm doing to him," I said. He couldn't hide the scowl on his face.

"I'm not going to feel any type of way for loving and wanting my family. He can't have what belongs to me. I need to go back to my room, shower and pack. I'll be back to take us to the airport," he said standing up. He walked out the room without looking back at me.

A few hours later, we all arrived at the airport. Even Yella Boy and Zuri were joining us. I was excited about this trip. Echon hasn't said much to me since he left my room earlier. I guess he didn't like the fact that I felt some kind of way about hurting Emmanuel. I couldn't help having compassion. We boarded Bull's private plane and were ready for takeoff.

"What the fuck?" Zelda asked looking ahead as she sat in her seat. I followed her eyes to see Jedrek getting on the plane.

He walked to the seats where Zelda was sitting. "Get up. I'm sitting by the window."

"No fuck you not, unless you sit somewhere else," she said with an attitude.

Dear, Vanity 2: Echon's Return   Nona Day

I don't know what was in the look he gave her, but she reluctantly got up and let him in to have the window seat. She flopped down in the aisle seat angrily. I giggled as she rolled her eyes at him. She closed her eyes and exhaled when he reached over and massaged her bare thigh while looking out the window. Yea, he was definitely in control.

Zelda

I don't know if I was mad or happy to see him. He has no right to demand I do as he say. Just the lust in his eyes for me makes me do everything he says. I could feel my wetness between my thighs from his hand on my thighs. He fell asleep with his hand still on my thigh. He tightened his grip when I tried to move his hand to go to the bathroom.

"I need to use the bathroom," I said nudging him. He looked at me with his sleepy eyes sliding his hand farther between my thighs. I needed to wipe the wetness spilling out of me.

"Bring yo ass right back," he said moving his hand.

"Nigga we in the air. Where I'm gone go?" I said rolling my eyes at him as I stood up.

He slapped me on the ass. "Don't get smart Zelly." *Stupid ass pet name.* I thought in my head but didn't speak out loud.

I was so happy we didn't fly commercial. The bathroom was beautiful, clean and smelled fresh. After relieving my bladder and washing my hands, I returned to my seat. I looked around to see everyone was asleep. When

I return to my seat, Jedrek was massaging his knee. I could tell by his facial expression he was in pain.

"Get up and stretch if your legs getting stiff," I advised him.

"Old injury," he said.

"I have some Tylenol," I said reaching for my bag. He declined the pills even though it was obvious he was in pain.

"What happened...to your knee?" I asked.

A solemn look covered his face. "I was shot in it."

My eyes grew big. This is why I didn't want a relationship with a street hustler, gang banger or anything similar. Their lives are in constant danger. I didn't want to sit home every night wondering if my boyfriend or husband is going to come home or if I'll be making a trip to the morgue to identify him.

"How did you get shot?" I asked.

"By a damn gun. Get up I gotta go piss," he said angrily.

"I don't understand you. You act like you don't like me one minute, the next you do. Why?" I asked not moving.

"Because you got the best pussy I ever had. Like I said, until my dick stops getting hard from thinking about you, I'm going to continue fucking you rather I like you or not," he stated.

"You are a fuckin' asshole," I said angrily standing up and taking my ass to another seat. I refuse to let him ruin this trip for me. I'm going to find me a fine ass island man to make me forget how good he fucks me.

A few hours later, we were checking in our rooms at the most exquisite resort in Montego Bay. I hurried off to my room. I wanted to get as far away from him as possible. The room was absolutely beautiful. I was exhausted from the flight. I couldn't wait to take a long, hot shower and crash. The sliding glass doors opened to a huge patio that had the most amazing view. I was going to wake up early just to see the sunrise. I stepped out on the balcony and took in the fresh air. I could smell the ocean water from the slight breeze. I went to answer the door when I heard a knock. I thought it was the bellman bringing up my

Dear, Vanity 2: Echon's Return   Nona Day

luggage. I opened the door to see Jedrek standing with my luggage. He waltzed in like always.

"What are you doing?" I asked as he dropped my bags. I noticed he also had his bags with him.

"I'm staying in here with you," he said pulling off his tee shirt.

"No hell you are not. I'm tired of you treating me like some kind of hoe. I wouldn't give a damn if you catch blue balls. You are not staying here and I'm not having sex with you anymore," I stated firmly.

He walked up to me and stared down at me. "How do you want me to treat you?"

I desperately wanted to answer that question, but I wasn't going to put myself out there to be broken. Not by him. I don't think this man has an emotional bone in his body.

"I don't want you to treat me like anything. I want you to forget you ever met me," I told him.

He scoffed. "A'ight, but I'm still staying here. All the rooms are booked up."

"Well, take yo ass to another hotel. I have plans while I'm here," I said turning to walk away from him.

He grabbed my arm and pulled me into his chest. The frown on his face almost scared me. "Plans like what?"

I decided to see if I could get under his skin the way he does mine. "To fuck me an island man."

He laughed in my face. "Go ahead. I'll make myself scarce when the time comes. I'm going to take a shower." He walked away leaving me more heated with anger. I started unpacking my clothes. We were only here for two days, but I bought enough for an entire week. I went to answer the door when I heard EJ's voice on the other side. He rushed in the room excited.

"We going to play football on the beach. Where's Drek?" He asked.

"Who told you Jedrek was in my room?"

He laughed. "Daddy. He told me to come get him from yo room." Before I could reply Jedrek walked out the bathroom with nothing, but a towel wrapped around his waist. EJ looked at me and smiled.

Dear, Vanity 2: Echon's Return   Nona Day

"Drek, Daddy said come to the beach. We met some kids my age. We gonna play football with them," he said.

"I'll be down in a few," Jedrek said to me. EJ hurried out the room as fast as he came in.

"You shouldn't be playing football on that knee. It's too stiff after that flight," I warned him.

"Why you care?"

"I don't," I replied before walking passed him and into the bathroom to take a shower and slip on my bikini.

*****

"I don't think Drek likes you flirting with those guys," Zuri said smiling as we lounged on the beach. I know he didn't. That's exactly why I was doing it. I'll show him better than I can tell him. That fine ass island nigga going to get these cookies tonight. So what if he was only twenty. I'm here for fun only.

"Zee knows exactly what she's doing. She's trying to get a reaction out of him," Vanity said rolling her eyes at me.

"Mind your business Van," I said rolling mine back at her. She laughed.

Dear, Vanity 2: Echon's Return   Nona Day

"Drek is a nice guy. He's just like Yella Boy. He's too damn blunt with his words. It must run in the family," Nika said laughing.

"Hey, get off my man. He is sweet as he can be…well, sometimes," Zuri said smiling.

"Forget Jedrek. I got other plans tonight. One of y'all better be making room in your room tonight for him, or he'll be sleeping on the beach," I said waltzing away to the bar.

I glanced over my shoulder and caught Jedrek staring at me. I put an extra twist in my walk, just so he could watch my ass. I sat at the bar flirting with the young Jamaican. Every time I glanced at Jedrek he was peering at me. He couldn't concentrate on playing football for watching me. That's exactly what I wanted. I couldn't keep my eyes off his dark chocolate, muscular, sweaty body. I jumped off the stool when I saw him fall as he ran with the football. I saw the grinch in his face. I knew he shouldn't have been playing on that stiff knee. I ran over to make sure he was okay. Yella Boy and Echon were helping him up as I rushed over.

Dear, Vanity 2: Echon's Return   Nona Day

"Are you okay?" I asked frantically. It was obvious he was in pain. He ignored me.

"You good?" Yella Boy asked him.

"Yea, I'm out," he said limping away. I watched him walk back into the hotel and I followed behind him. I got on the elevator with him.

"The fuck you following me for?" He asked.

"Because I have the damn key to the room you idiot," I said staring up at him.

"Give it here and take yo hoe ass back on the beach," he spewed.

I smiled on the inside because I know he was jealous. He got off the elevator limping. I followed behind him with a smile on my face. When we got in the room, he flopped down on the sofa. I wrapped some ice in a towel and sat next to him placing the towel on his knee. I didn't have a clue if this would help, but I figured it wouldn't hurt.

"Vanity keeps pain killers with her. She can give you something," I said softly.

"Thanks," he said holding the towel over his knee.

Dear, Vanity 2: Echon's Return   Nona Day

"You're welcome. I'll call her and tell her to bring some to the room," I said dialing her number.

"You ain't gotta sit up here with me. I'm good," he said glancing at me.

"I was getting bored anyway. Plus it's too hot," I lied shrugging my shoulders. I wanted to be near him and then again, I didn't. I don't know what I was feeling for him. I shouldn't be feeling anything, because all we've ever done was have sex. Best sex of my life, but it was still just sex between us. He sat quietly for a few minutes before he spoke.

"I was coming home from football practice one night. I saw this man beating the shit out of this girl in the middle of the street. No one would stop him. He was some big time drug dealer. I beat the shit out of him. A couple of days later, he caught me walking home from practice. Him and a few guys beat me almost to death before shooting me in the knee. It was enough damage to destroy my chances of going pro. I had scholarship offers from all the top schools. After I got shot, none of them were willing to take a chance on me with my injury," he explained. Even though it didn't show on his face, I saw the hurt in his eyes.

"I'm sorry. Is that why you started selling drugs?" I asked.

"Who the fuck said I sell drugs. Don't speak on shit you know nothing about," he said furiously. I sucked my teeth, scooted to the far end of the couch and folded my arms. Every time I think we might be connecting, he reminds me we aren't. Silence filled the room again. I was just torturing myself by sitting here with him.

He cleared his throat. "I didn't need football to go to college. I wanted to play football, because it's what I loved. I scored high enough on my SAT to get into all the schools that took their scholarships away, but I wasn't financially able to pay for them. So, I did what I had to do to pay for college."

"You went to college?" I asked shocked.

He scoffed. "Yea, a street nigga with a MBA." I couldn't help but smile.

"Prop your leg up on the sofa. I'm going to go down and get the pills from Van," I said getting up.

Dear, Vanity 2: Echon's Return   Nona Day

"You better bring yo hot ass right back," he said as I walked to the door. I smiled as I made my way out the door.

Echon

I could feel the tension between me and Vanity. She was stressing over breaking things off with Emmanuel, and I was stressing because I couldn't stand the fact that she has feelings for him. I know I had no right to be upset. She had to move on with her life, but I couldn't help it. I was here now, and didn't like sharing her heart. We spent the entire day with the kids. We had just got back to the room from having dinner. I had my own room, because we didn't want to confuse EJ. My meeting was with Chiraq in the morning. I was relieved I didn't have to make up an excuse about my whereabouts, since all the ladies were going shopping. Since Fiji came with us, he was in the room with EJ and Baby Gladys playing. They had her just as tough as them. She thought she was one of the boys. I walked in Vanity's room and she was trying to unzip her dress. I walked up behind her and unzipped her dress. I held her hands down by her side and placed kisses on her shoulder.

"Every night I'm scared to go to sleep. I feel like I'm going to wake up from this dream," she said softly.

I wrapped my arms around her waist and held her tight. "It's not a dream Vanity. I'm here and I'm not going anywhere."

She turned around to face me. "I don't love him. I want to be with you. It's just that I have compassion for him. He loves me, and I have to tell him I want to be with you. I've never had to hurt anyone like that."

I kissed her lips softly. "I understand. I'm sorry for getting upset with you. I just don't like the thought of sharing your heart."

"Even in your death, my heart only belonged to you," she said.

"Let's just enjoy this trip. We'll worry about Ernest later," I said purposely getting his name wrong. She laughed and nudged my shoulder.

"I better put on some clothes, before one of the kids come running in here," she said.

"I'm going to my room to change. I'll be back. We taking them down on the beach to build a fire. They want to make smores," I said smiling.

Dear, Vanity 2: Echon's Return   Nona Day

She propped her hand on one hip. "I think you are enjoying being a kid more than EJ." I chuckled because it was true. I never got to do the things as a child I'm doing with my son. I was walking out the room when EJ stopped me.

"Daddy where you going? I want you to stay in the room with us," he asked sadly.

"I'm going to my room to change. Y'all said y'all wanted to build a fire and make smores didn't you?" I asked. He shouted with joy and ran back to his bedroom to tell the others.

An hour later, we were out on the beach making smores. Vanity told the kids campfire stories. This is the life I thought I could never have with her. No one or nothing was going to take this away from us. After the fire went out, we went back upstairs. I stayed until we put them to bed. Me and Vanity made our way to her bedroom making sure to lock the door behind us. She made love to me that left me in a world filled with rainbows and unicorns.

Dear, Vanity 2: Echon's Return   Nona Day

*****

The next morning all the ladies left with the kids to spend the day out shopping. I met Tree, Yella Boy and Drek down in the lobby. Chiraq had a limo waiting out front to take us to his estate. Dose had called him to let him know we would be coming to visit him. I knew Chiraq well from being Bull's shadow. He was one of the real ones left in the game. I know if he knew anything, I could trust it's real. We drove down a long deserted road filled with nothing but palm trees. At the end of the road sat his heavily guarded mansion. We rode through the double gated doors and parked in front of the mansion. Chiraq stood outside waiting for our arrival. When we got out the car, he smiled as we walked up to him.

"I'll be damn, you live," he said smiling at me. He embraced me with a tight, brotherly hug.

"Come," he said walking to the tall, double doors of his mansion. The entire mansion was decorated with African style art. We followed him through the mansion and outside on his pool deck where a feast fit for a king was prepared.

"Enjoy the food," he said as we sat around a long table. All of us starting pigging out on the food. It was all

Dear, Vanity 2: Echon's Return   Nona Day

Jamaican food. I had the best curry goat I've ever eaten. I didn't touch the steak, because it was still bleeding. I grimaced as I watched Yella Boy cut into his ribeye steak.

Chiraq kept staring at me. I knew I was going to have to tell him how I was sitting at his table right now. I decided to go ahead and get it over with. I'm starting to feel like a broken record. He sat quietly and listened. His eyes glazed at me in disbelief. I don't know what it was, but it looked as if he wanted to cry.

"We thought you were dead," was all he said after I was done. I guess he still wasn't over me being alive.

"Yea, we've established that," Drek said. He was definitely Yella Boy's cousin. They said whatever came to their minds.

"No, I mean when your parents were killed, we thought their twin boys were killed also. Me and Bull's father searched for you and your brother. We couldn't find you. I can't believe you are here," he said.

"Is what my uncle told me the truth?" He asked.

"Partially. Bull's father didn't find out about your father's death until after it happened. Some of the younger members wanted to change the legacy rules. That was one of the main reasons he wanted to dismantle the families. Me, your father, and Bull's father were best friends. They killed Bull's father when he decided to dismantle the families after your parent's death. That's when Sanchez took over," he informed us. I was relieved to know Bull's father had nothing to do with my parent's death. He went on to tell us everything he knew.

"I found my uncle dead. I think his son killed him. He's turned my uncle's own militia army against him. He's taken over Bull's cocoa fields and raged war in the streets," I told him. His eyes widened.

"The militia was never your uncle's. Your father built that army. They only obeyed your uncle because he is your father's brother. Your uncle's son is claiming your legacy. The legacy is yours. All you need to do is find the leader of the militia. He's the only one that can make them stand down. You have to prove to him you're the one that rules," he said. He was telling me too damn much. I didn't want to rule a damn thing. All I wanted was to stop my cousin and have my life with Vanity and EJ. I didn't care anything about owning a legacy.

"How the hell we find the leader?" Tree asked.

"I already know who the leader is," I said. They all looked at me for the answer.

"My uncle kept one person by his side at all times. Thomas must've turned her against my uncle. Her name is Shavonna," I said.

"How we supposed to find her?" Yella Boy asked.

"I don't know. I need to go back to the house. I'm sure my uncle has some information on her in his study," I said.

Tree answered his phone when it rang. "Nika you gotta fuckin' calm down. I can't understand you." He sat quietly for a few seconds before his eyes zeroed in on me. I panicked thinking something happened to Vanity and EJ. I immediately jumped up.

"They're okay," he said standing up to calm me down. I exhaled a deep sigh of relief.

"What happened?" Drek asked.

SOUL Publications

Dear, Vanity 2: Echon's Return   Nona Day

"That big dude you used to run with in the A. He called Vanity and told her the nigga she seeing was shot multiple times. He's still alive, but it's not looking good. Nika said Vanity freaking out. She's trying to book a flight home. She thinks its tied to you," he said.

I stretched my eyes. "She thinks I did it?"

He shrugged his shoulders. "I don't know fam. I just know Nika said she's scared and wants to go home."

Vanity

Icouldn't think straight as I threw all my clothes in my suitcase. I felt like this was all my fault. Emmanuel is a good man. He didn't have any enemies. This has to be connected to Echon. I refuse to let myself believe that Echon would do something like this even though the thought crossed my mind.

"Mama, why we gotta leave? We having fun," EJ asked as I packed.

"Emmanuel has been hurt. I need to go be with him," I told him.

"Okay, I'll go pack my things," he said sadly walking out the room with his head down.

I know he didn't want to leave but I had to go. I couldn't continue to stay here in paradise while Emmanuel was fighting for his life. Zelda pleaded with me to wait for Echon to come back. I was furious with him for pretending this was a family vacation. This was all a business trip for him to seek revenge for Bull. I wanted to get away from all this craziness. After grabbing me and EJ's luggage, I headed toward the elevator with Zelda behind me pleading for me to stay. She followed us down to the lobby where a shuttle was waiting to take us to the airport.

"Don't let her leave with him! She's trying to kidnap my son!" Zelda screamed as I rushed through the lobby. I stopped and turned to face her with an open mouth. I can't believe she said that. EJ thought it was all a joke. He couldn't stop laughing. Security came up to me and asked for identification that Echon was my son.

"Those IDs are fake! You have to believe me!" Zelda cried faking tears.

"Ma'am we will need to verify this is your son," the hotel security said.

"Are you serious?" I asked looking at him in disbelief.

"We just need to verify this is your son," he tried explaining.

"Ask him. He's old enough to answer," I told him pointing at EJ as he laughed nonstop.

"Just follow me," he said. I huffed and gave Zelda a look that could kill. She only grinned and licked her tongue out at me. I grabbed EJ's hand and followed the man to the hotel security office.

Dear, Vanity 2: Echon's Return   Nona Day

I sat in an empty room while the officer took EJ with him. I prayed EJ didn't go along with Zelda's crazy story. I had been in the room for nearly an hour. I was getting impatient and frustrated. I jumped up when the door open. EJ came in licking an ice cream cone.

"Sorry, but we had to make sure," the officer said sincerely.

"Come on, EJ," I said walking out the room. Zelda got what she wanted. Echon was pacing the floor of the lobby when we got there.

"Daddy, Aunt Zee played a trick on Mama. She's so funny," EJ said running up to Echon. It still melted my heart to see them together.

"Do me a favor and go over there and play with Fiji and Baby Gladys while I talk to your mom," he said kneeling down to him. EJ hurried away.

Echon stood there staring at me. "What are you doing Vanity?"

"I'm going home to be by a friend's side. What if all this craziness is the reason he was shot? What if whoever tried to kill Bull thinks he's tied up in all this? He was at the hotel with you in my room. Maybe they think he's involved in whatever is going on. This could all be my fault. I called him to come there," I ranted.

He walked up to me. "And if all this is true, you think taking our son back there is safe?" I hated to admit it, but he was right. I wasn't thinking rationally.

"I just can't stay here while he's there fighting for his life. The least I can do is be there for him," I explained.

He started twisting his coils. "Fine. I'll go with you. EJ can stay here."

"I can't leave my son," I said.

"*Our* son is safer here and staying in New Orleans for now. I know he'll be protected," he said. I didn't mean to make it seem like EJ's well-being wasn't his concern.

"I'm sorry. I didn't mean it the way it sounded," I said.

"I know. Let me go pack my things and we'll take the jet back," he said calmly.

"How are they going to get back?" I asked.

Dear, Vanity 2: Echon's Return   Nona Day

"The jet will come back and pick them up," he assured me. I nodded my head.

When he came back down, we explained everything to EJ. He didn't care about us leaving. He was too excited he was staying. I trusted Tree and Yella Boy to protect our son. Zelda apologized for what she did. Even though I was mad at her, I couldn't help but laugh at her drastic measures.

*****

Atlanta, Ga

I was glad I left my car parked at the airport. We went straight to the hospital. I hurried to the ICU floor with Echon by my side. I realized I didn't think things through before bringing Echon here. One of the reasons I liked Emmanuel was because he was family oriented. He was very close to his family, especially his twin sister, Emory. When we stepped off the elevator, we came face to face with her. She gave me a look that could kill.

"You have the audacity to show your face here?" She asked mean mugging me.

Dear, Vanity 2: Echon's Return   Nona Day

"I-I just found it. I just wanted to be here for him," I said shamefully. It dawned on me how bad this looks with Echon standing beside me.

She laughed. "I've been talking to my brother. I know who this is. I don't give a damn about him coming back from the dead. You waltz your ass in here like you give a damn about Em. If you did, you wouldn't be standing here with him. He's probably the reason Em is laying there fighting for his life."

Echon stepped in her space. "I know this a rough time for you. You can come at me with all your emotions, but not her."

"Nigga, get the fuck out my face and take her with you," she spewed glancing at me. I glanced at Echon and saw the craziness in his eyes. I remembered him cutting that boy's throat that tried to attack me. I pulled him back and stood face to face with Emory.

"Regardless of what you may think of me, I care about Emmanuel. I can care less what you think of me. I will see him rather you like it or not," I stated.

"Try to move me," she said daring me.

Dear, Vanity 2: Echon's Return   Nona Day

I scoffed. "You either move or I tell your husband where you spend all your Sunday's after church while he goes home to watch football." Her eyes widened.

"Yea, I know. Now move, or I will unleash him on you," I said with a devilish grin. The way Echon was looking at her she knew that wouldn't be a good thing.

She stood still. "He's not going in there." I looked over at Echon and he nodded his head. I moved passed her bumping her shoulders.

The waiting room was full of his family members. Everyone gave me the same look as Emory. I ignored them. I know it wasn't a good idea for him to sit in there with them. I asked him to wait downstairs in the lobby. He gave me a look of disapproval. I know he felt like he needed to be near me to protect me from them. I explained to him he taught me to stand for myself, and not to live my life other's people's opinion. I could handle whatever they had to say to me. I know God knows my heart better than I do.

His parents were in his room. I was surprised when they welcomed me in the room. They gave me a comforting hug and left me in the room with Emmanuel. It broke my heart to see him hooked to all the machines. The ventilator

Dear, Vanity 2: Echon's Return   Nona Day

was keeping him alive. Only God's grace and mercy could save him. I sat by his bed holding his hand praying God will pull him through. After saying my prayer, I asked for his forgiveness. I started talking to him sharing memories that we shared together. Even though my heart was with Echon, Emmanuel was a blessing to have in my life. I didn't want to consume too much time from his family, so I promised him I would be back tomorrow.

When I got downstairs, Echon was sitting in the waiting area patiently waiting for me. He looked into my eyes to make sure I was okay. If I wasn't, I would pretend to be to save any one of Emmanuel's family from his wrath. I fell asleep on the way back to the house. I awakened next to him in the bed we never shared together in the home he left me. I felt his arm around my waist as he spooned me. A feeling of happiness consumed me having him here with me. I slipped out of bed without waking him. I took care of my morning hygiene and slipped on a cool summer dress. I made a mental note to go get my hair done later today. The salt water from the beach ruined my current style. I felt the need for some faux locs. I was in the kitchen cooking breakfast when the doorbell rang. I looked at my phone to see who it was. I went and opened the door for Quran. He followed me to the kitchen. He sat at the isle while I cooked breakfast.

"Have you went to the hospital?" He asked.

"Yes, I went straight there when we landed. Emory and most of the family wasn't happy to see me, but his parents were welcoming," I said turning to face him.

"Well, you have to understand why she's upset," he said.

"I understand but that wasn't the time or place. I was there as a friend. Whatever feelings she has for me could've waited.

"Emmanuel told her things about Echon. She thinks he has something to do with it," he said.

I thought for a few seconds. I never told Emmanuel things about Echon. How did he know about Echon's past?

Guilt covered his face. "He has a right to know. He only wants what's best for you and EJ."

"How dare you Quran? You have no right. Echon would never do anything like that. If he did, he would do it himself and you know that," I stated.

"You sure about that Vanity. It's been a long time. People change," he said.

I walked over to the isle. "What are you trying to say?" I didn't like where he was going with this conversation.

"All I'm saying is I know you still love him, but is it worth risking you and EJ's life. He hasn't been back a full week and he's already deep in some shit. How long do you think it will be before it's at your front doorstep?"

"He will protect us with his life," I replied.

He shook his head. "Aren't you supposed to be a woman of God. Look how you've changed since he's been back in your life. You are hurting a man that loves you by cheating on him."

I became angry. "Don't' judge me Quran. I don't live my life by people's opinions and perspectives of how to love and serve our God. My relationship with him in monogamous. He knows my heart, mind and soul."

My eyes met Echon's when he walked into the kitchen. I hoped he didn't hear what Quran said, but by the look in his eyes I know he did. I glanced at Quran and saw the shock on his face. Echon looked at him and gave him a head nod. The tension between them could be cut with a knife.

"If you want EJ here with you, I will go get him," Echon said.

I didn't want to ruin his vacation. I know how much he enjoys being with Fiji and Baby Gladys. "We can call him and see what he wants to do."

He leaned down and kissed my lips softly before giving Quran his attention. I thought he was going to get in Quran's behind for what he said, but he didn't. He made small talk with him. Quran told him all about how we worked together and cleaned up the blocks. They talked as I prepared breakfast like the conversation between me and Quran never happened. I think Echon was trying to bond again with his old friend. Quran seemed to be happy as the talked and laughed. I felt good seeing them together like old times.

Zelda

"Get up!" Jedrek barked smacking me on the ass. I guess he was still mad I made him sleep on the sofa. We were being cordial with each other, but I was determined not to have sex with him again. The more time I spent with him the more I liked him. That wasn't a good thing. I know this nigga will break my heart.

"I ain't fucking you! Leave me alone," I said pulling the cover over my head.

"If I wanted to fuck you, I would with your permission. Now, get up!" He said yanking the cover off of me.

"Ugh! What do you want?" I screamed jumping up and standing up in the bed. I was beyond pissed. We went to a club together last night while Zuri and Yella Boy watched the kids. I had a huge hangover from all the shots I drank. I had the best time with him trying to get to know him outside of the bedroom. He's nice and fun when he's intoxicated and high.

He laughed. "Put on some clothes and meet me downstairs." He walked toward the door.

"It's not even daylight. Where the fuck are we going?" I asked angrily. He walked out the door ignoring my question.

All of a sudden, I panicked. I remembered all the craziness that happened with Vanity yesterday. I didn't bother to get dressed. I threw my silk robe over my panties and rushed downstairs. I grabbed my phone to see what time it was. It was approximately six o'clock. Something had to be wrong for him to pull me out of bed this early. He was standing in the lobby when I stepped off the elevator.

"What's wrong? Is Vanity okay? Where's EJ?" I asked frantically. Without answering my questions he grabbed my hand and led me out the back of the hotel that lead to the beach.

"Where are we going? What's going on?" I asked as he pulled me farther down on the beach. Still, no reply.

My heart melted when I saw the direction we were going. There was a blanket with lit candles and breakfast for two. I stood there staring down at the beautiful arrangement in awe. I looked at him as he looked up at the sky.

"You said you wanted to see the sunrise. This a better view than the balcony. Now, sit down," he said.

I smiled and sat down on the blanket while he sat across from me. We sat and ate the Jamaican breakfast quietly. My eyes roamed over his chiseled abdomen as I tried not to think of him sliding inside me.

"The sun is starting to come up. You need to sit on this side if you want a good view," he said. I scooted to his side of the blanket. He stood up and sat behind me with his legs opened. I couldn't resist resting against his broad chest.

We sat and watched the sunrise like a picture perfect couple. "Only God could create such beauty," I said fascinated by the beautiful sun rising.

He slipped his hand inside my robe cupping my breast. My body shivered when he stroked his thumb over my hard nipple. He starting giving my neck soft, wet kisses. He slid his other hand inside my panties. While massaging my breast, licking on my neck and earlobe, he played in my wetness as it poured from me.

"Aaaaahhh!" I moaned when he slipped two fingers inside me. He massaged my clit while sliding his fingers in and out of me. I started winding my hips as the pleasure of his handy work sent tingling chills through my body.

"You ready to come?" he asked. His fingers twirled inside me until he found my spot. He repeatedly brought me to the edge only to pull me back. I couldn't take the teasing he was doing to me. I pleaded with him to let me come. I thrust my hips as he teased my spot. He pressed against my soft spot. My body stiffened as my eyes rolled to the back of my head. I clinched my thighs trapping his hand praying he would let me release. I exploded all over his hand.

"Yea, that's it. Make that pussy cream," he moaned in my ear.

My body shivered relentlessly until he pulled his fingers from inside me. He ran his fingertips over my bottom lip before sucking my creaminess from his fingers. I slowly sat myself up turning around to straddle his lap.

Dear, Vanity 2: Echon's Return   Nona Day

With a passionate, wet kiss I pulled his rock hard dick from his grey sweats. He gripped a handful of my hair, biting, sucking and moaning on my neck as I slid down his dick.

"Fuuuck!" He groaned from the ecstasy of being inside me.

I wrapped my hands around his neck and started riding him with no mercy. He licked and sucked my hard nipples and he massaged my breasts. Another orgasm ripped through my body, but I didn't stop. For the first time I was in control of him. His groans and grunts only made me go harder. I planted the soles of my feet into the blanket and bounced up and down on his cream coated dick. He gripped my ass cheeks trying to slow me down, but I felt myself getting ready to come again. His dick starting swelling and throbbing inside me. I wanted to make him come at my will the same way he does me.

"I wanna feel you come inside me. Come with me Jedrek," I moaned seductively in his ear.

"Sssshhhit! Yo pussy so mothafuckin' good!" He groaned. My pet name never sounded so damn good as he moaned it in my ear.

Dear, Vanity 2: Echon's Return   Nona Day

I held his face between my hands stroking my tongue over his lips before sucking his tongue in my mouth. I was grinding on his dick as we moaned and groaned. I started rocking back and forth as he slid in and out of me. When I heard that familiar grunt he makes before he explodes I went crazy on his dick.

"Aaaaaaarrrrggghhhh! Got dammmnnnn!" He roared so deep and loud that it could possibly cause ripples in the ocean.

I exploded with him feeling as if I was connected with an magnetic force. Our sweaty bodies clung to each other as I collapsed in his arms. We sat there for the longest just holding each other. The cool breeze made my body shiver. He wrapped the extra blanket around me and stood up with me still straddling him. His dick was still hard inside me. I could feel it pulsating against my walls. He carried me to the elevator. Once we stepped inside the elevator, he started drilling inside me again. He didn't stop until the elevator stopped. Once inside the room, we christened the hotel room and balcony. When he was done with me, I was laying on the bed in a fetal position

Dear, Vanity 2: Echon's Return   Nona Day

shivering form the electric sensations traveling through my nerves.

"Zelly," he said softly reaching over and stroking my flesh. I couldn't stand the touch of his fingertips. My body quivered and locked up.

"Please don't touch me," I pleaded softly. My body felt like it was being electrified with waves of unexplainable force.

He chuckled. "We have to get ready. The plane will be leaving in a couple of hours."

A couple of hours later, we were on our way back to New Orleans. This was a vacation I would never forget. I kept telling myself I wasn't in love with him. It was only lust and mind blowing sex. I barely knew him. There was no way I could be in love with him. I'm smart and strong enough not to believe falling in love is this easy, but every thought of him made my heart pound. I needed to prove to myself I didn't fall in love with a man I hardly knew because of sex.

EJ went home with Tree and Nika. He wanted to stay the remainder of his vacation. I decided to stay a couple of more days to enjoy the culture before I leave. I was surprised when Jedrek said he was staying with me. When we got back to the hotel, he cooked dinner for us. We lounged around the room actually enjoying each other's company. He wasn't making it easy to not love him. He answered his phone when Yella Boy called. I could tell by his conversation he was getting ready to go somewhere.

"I'll be back tomorrow. I gotta go handle some business," he said standing up.

"Tomorrow? Where are you going? You just gone leave me here by myself with no explanation?" I asked following him to the door.

He turned to face me. "I don't owe you shit. If you don't wanna stay here, take yo ass back to Atlanta." Once again, he reminds me why I don't like him.

"Don't bother coming back nigga. I don't want you here," I said turning to walk away. He followed me to the bedroom and grabbed his luggage. He walked out the room without another word.

Echon

"Thanks for breakfast. I gotta get going. Got some business to handle," Quran said standing from the barstool. Vanity gave him a half smile. I could tell she was still upset about the conversation they had. At first, I thought Quran was just being protective of Vanity the way I am. As we sat and ate breakfast, I realized what he couldn't hide.

"Let me ride with you," I said standing up and looking at him. He gave me an unsure stare.

Vanity looked horrified. "I thought we could spend the day together."

"Nah, you check on your friend. I need to catch up with Q," I stated as I started walking out the kitchen.

She stood in front of me blocking me from leaving the kitchen. "Quran, can you wait outside. I need to speak with Echon." He nodded his head and left the kitchen. Vanity peered up at me until she heard the front door shut.

"What are you going to do with him?" She asked.

Dear, Vanity 2: Echon's Return   Nona Day

I had no intentions of killing Quran. I have more respect and love for my brother now than before I left. He was there for Vanity and EJ when I wasn't. He stepped up when I left. He didn't have to be there for them, but he chose to because of the bond we had with each other. I just felt we needed to talk and say our peace. I know he has some feelings about the way I left.

"Nothing Vanity," I stated honestly.

"Don't kill him Echon. He's entitled to his opinion. He was there for me during a rough time," she reminded me.

"I know. For that reason, I would never harm him unless I'm forced to do so," I said.

Her shoulders relaxed. "With all the craziness going on. I forgot to tell you about the lounge you never opened." I arched my brow at her.

She smiled. "I opened it. Business is great. I have a staff running it. Me and Zelda help out on weekends sometimes. I wanted to take you there and surprise you, but you'll see it with Quran."

I smiled and winked at her. "I'd rather see it with you. I won't go near that area. I'll let you take me on a date tonight." She giggled and blushed. She tiptoed and kissed me softly on the lips before I left.

*****

"Where we going?" Quran asked as I hopped in the truck.

"Not the old blocks," I said. We rode in silence as I enjoyed being back in Atlanta. Out of all the places I lived, Atlanta and New Orleans felt like home. We rode until he pulled up to a car wash. I followed him inside as he tossed one of the workers the keys to his G-wagon. He stepped into an office. I guess this was one of his businesses he started up since I've been gone. Based on all the cars in the parking lot, business is good.

"I see you made shit happen when I left. Proud of you," I said as I took a seat in front of his desk. He nodded and sat behind his desk. Someone tapped on the door and walked in. A thick chick with more ass than Serena Williams walked in. She sashayed over to the desk and placed some invoices on the table. She turned to face me.

Dear, Vanity 2: Echon's Return   Nona Day

"Damn Q, who is this?" She asked him never taking her eyes off me. I chuckled as she roamed over me like I was the last supper for her.

"None of yo got damn business. Now, get the fuck out. Yo hoe ass try to fuck every nigga come through here," he stated angrily. I could see the embarrassment on her face. She stormed out of the room.

"Damn, that's you or something?" I asked not sure why he was getting so angry with her.

"I fucked a few times. She will fuck a dog to bust a nut," he said.

I laughed. "That's the kind you like." He didn't laugh with me.

"Nah, I used to," he stated firmly. I nodded my head and stopped laughing.

"It's obvious you got some kind of animosity toward me. Get it off your chest, because you just used your one and only spare my life card back at the house," I said eyeing him.

"Oh, niggas die for speaking the truth?" He asked sarcastically.

Dear, Vanity 2: Echon's Return   Nona Day

I leaned forward to make sure he understood me. "I know I left in a fucked up way. If I had it to do over, I would. I didn't come to you because I knew you would convince me to stay. I give you all the respect and love in this world for what you did for Vanity and EJ. I'm indebted to you for the rest of my life. With that being said, don't ever try to come between me and her. Your opinion of our relationship isn't needed. Whatever feelings you have about me and her take it to your grave."

He glared back at me. "And when the bullshit you involved in almost destroys her. I'll be there to pick up the bullshit she's left with." There was no doubt about his feelings for her.

I leaned back in the chair never looking away from him. "When did you fall in love with her?"

"Man, gone with that bullshit. You got what you want. You feel threatened or something because of my relationship with her and EJ?" He asked.

"Nah, maybe somewhat jealous of how highly my son speaks of you. I want you to keep that relationship with him. I want you to keep your friendship with Vanity. If being only her friend isn't possible for you, you need to find a way to deal with it," I said.

"You know my gun shoots just like yours," he said with a smirk.

I chuckled. "So, you want to kill me over my pussy? You was letting another nigga dick her down while I was gone." A scowl appeared on his face. I didn't want this conversation to get this heated, but I wasn't feeling him right now.

"His time with her was only temporary. He wasn't a threat. I'm the only one that's willing to accept that she will never get over you," he stated boldly. I respected Quran for not lying to my face. He wasn't going to deny his feelings for her.

He leaned forward resting his elbows on his desk. "I'm not going to deny what can't be denied when you see it with your own eyes. What I said to her back at the house isn't about my feelings though. If I stood any chance with her, it ended with your return. It's about her and EJ's safety. You left one dangerous life to go to another. Before I let you pull them in that world, we will go to war."

"Understood," I said holding my hand out. He shook my hand. I didn't know how this would play out with him having feelings for her. I understood how easy it was to fall in love with her. This is my brother that supported and loved my family when I wasn't here. Hopefully this won't tear us apart.

*****

Things felt a little awkward between me and Quran for a few hours. Just like men, we went back to being our normal selves. The way I saw it, we both knew our place. We spoke truth and respected each other's side of the coin. I didn't visit the lounge like I told Vanity. I got the phone number for the lounge and planned something nice for our date tonight. When I got home, she was in the bedroom getting dressed. I walked up behind her wrapping my arms around her waist. She shivered as I kissed her from her neck to her shoulder.

"I like the bedroom," I whispered in her ear as I nibbled on her earlobe. Without realizing it, my hand was jacking up her knee length, backless dress. She gently grabbed my hand and turned to face me.

"I didn't want our memories to fade away. I tried duplicating your apartment. Every time I tried changing things in the house to move on with my life, I couldn't. When I finally did, I decorated based on simplicity," she said smiling at me.

"I'm home now Vanity. When things settle down, we'll buy a new house and you can decorate with whatever colors you like," I said.

"No, I don't want a new house. This is our house. I mean don't let me stop you if you want to buy us a second one, but this is our home," she said smiling. I chuckled.

"Now, shower and get dressed while I finish," she said walking away. She sat down at her vanity mirror to apply the small amount of makeup she normally wears.

"I'm sorry for leaving you Vanity," I said looking through the mirror at her.

She glared back at me. "I know Echon. You're home now. That's all that matters to me. Now, hurry up."

Four Days Later

Zelda

e and EJ arrived back in Atlanta early this morning. He was ready to come home to see his daddy, so we cut the vacation short by a couple of days. Jedrek hasn't called or texted me since he left me in New Orleans. Then again, he never does. He just shows up, gets what he wants from me and leaves like I was nothing to him. Today, me and Vanity was out shopping while EJ enjoyed time with his father.

"So, have you sat down and talked with EJ about your relationship with Echon?" I asked her as we sat in the food court.

"We're doing it tonight. I don't know why I'm so nervous. Being judged by adults doesn't bother me, but I couldn't handle it from my child," she said.

I laughed. "Why would he judge you?"

"I was just in a relationship with Emmanuel. Now, I'm going to tell him I love his father. How do I explain that to a child?" She asked.

Dear, Vanity 2: Echon's Return   Nona Day

"Vanity you are thinking too much. EJ is not going to think about any of that. He's going to be ecstatic about his parents being in love," I told her.

"I hope so," she replied nervously.

"Come on. I need to hit up Nordstrom's before we go. I saw this sexy ass skirt suit I want to buy for court tomorrow," I said standing up.

She giggled. "You should look professional in the court room not sexy."

"Not when the jury is full of perverted old men and middle aged bored white men," I said winking at her.

I found the skirt set I wanted and went to the dressing room to try it on. I hated my small waist most of the time. It didn't mesh with my thick thighs, wide hips and big ass. Most of my clothes had to be altered because they fitted in the hip and thigh area, but was too big in the waist. I had a personal tailor to correct them to my liking. Vanity browsed the store while I rushed to try on the outfit. I had just taken off my clothes when the dressing room door opened. I opened my mouth to scream, but Jedrek covered it gently pushing me against the mirrored wall. The way he stared at me made my pussy jump.

Dear, Vanity 2: Echon's Return   Nona Day

"I wanna taste you. Don't fuckin' scream," he mumbled in my ear.

The thought of his lips and tongue caressing my pussy made me forget he was bat shit crazy. He dropped to his knees pushing my thighs apart and rested them on his shoulders. He pushed my laced boy shorts to the side and stared up at me.

"Tell me I can taste you," he said in low, raspy tone. I wanted it so bad I couldn't speak. I gently grabbed the back of his head and pushed his face into my mound. Just the touch, feel and smell of him had me dripping wet.

"Open it for me," he demanded softly.

Without hesitation I spread my lips exposing my wetness. He started doing the weirdest shit, but it felt so good I felt myself getting ready to cum. He started massaging me with his face smearing my juices from his forehead to his chin. He was licking, sucking, nibbling, and slurping on me all at the same time. I tried to push his head away because I felt one of those earth shaking orgasms getting ready to come through me. He grunted letting me know he wasn't stopping. I folded my lips into my mouth to keep from screaming out loud.

Dear, Vanity 2: Echon's Return   Nona Day

"I'm going to scream," I pleaded with him.

Without taking a break from feasting on my soul, he gave me my shirt. I muffled my moans and whimpers with it. He slipped two to fingers inside my soaked tunnel as he vandalized my swollen clit with his tongue. I prayed to God to keep my sanity. I started bucking and twirling my hips. His groans and grunts were muffled inside my pussy. He slipped his tongue between my ass cheeks. It was unfair what he was doing to me, but my body couldn't resist him. Those electric vibrations racing through me from the tips of my toes to my heart as my mouth started to water. I couldn't hold it any longer. I exploded so hard I heard my essence gush from me and spatter against his face. I dropped my shirt and dug my nails into his shoulders. My body quivered and jerked as he sopped up every drop. I glanced down at him at work. His face glistened from my wetness with my creaminess saturated in his beard. Never have a man made me squirt and cream at the same time. When he was done, he sat me down in the chair in the dressing room. With sex induced eyes I looked up at him. He licked my remnants from his lips before wiping his mouth with the back of his hand like a savage animal. I wanted to hate and love him at the same time.

"I'll be back when I need some more," he said before walking out my dressing room. I sat there until the feeling came back in my legs. I quickly dressed and hurried out of the dressing room. Vanity was sitting in the dressing room's waiting area with a stupid ass grin on her face.

"Why would you allow him to come back there?" I said angrily.

She laughed. "Payback's a bitch. Remember you tried to get me arrested in Jamaica?"

"Fuck you Vanity!" I said sticking my middle finger up at her. She burst out laughing as I rushed out the store.

We rode silently until she spoke. "He's trying to break you from that hard ass exterior. He knows there's a softer you inside. Let him see it Zelda." I rolled my eyes at her, because she was right. I was scared to let him know how I felt.

She smiled at me. "I heard you."

"Look," I said holding up my nails. I had dug so deep in his flesh his skin was under my fingernails. She giggled. I've decided that was the last time I'm playing his game. I have to try something different with him.

Later that evening

I decided to try Vanity's approach by showing my softer side. I sent him a text inviting him to dinner at my home. He never replied back. That was typical of him. I slaved in the kitchen trying to cook. Vanity talked me through making lasagna over the phone. It looked good when I took it out the oven. I smiled and gave myself a pat on the back. After preparing dinner, I showered and dressed in a sexy nude colored dress that barely covered my ass. I guess he wasn't interested in seeing where this crazy thing between us can go. I fell asleep on the couch waiting for him. I awakened to my ringing doorbell. I was furious when I looked at my phone. It was almost midnight. I looked at the security monitor from my phone. He was standing on the other side of the door with his finger laying on my doorbell. I rushed to the door yanking it open.

"Get yo damn finger off my doorbell!" I demanded angrily.

He stepped inside without my permission. "Where you want it?"

Dear, Vanity 2: Echon's Return   Nona Day

"Want what?" I asked confused.

"My fingers," he said holding up the two fingers that helped put the fire out inside me earlier today.

I demanded he leave. Of course, he ignored me and went to the kitchen. He sat a bottle of wine on the table he had brought with him. He put foil over the pan of lasagna and put it back in the oven. I stood there watching him as he took control of the romantic evening I had planned for us.

"Where we eating? The kitchen or the dining room?" He asked opening the bottle of wine.

"Fix you a carry out plate. I have court in the morning. Good night," I said turning to go to my bedroom. I walked slow hoping he would stop me, but he didn't.

I undressed and slipped on a tank top and a pair of granny panties. I was going over documents when he came in the bedroom carrying a tray of the meal I prepared. He had taken a rose and candle from the dining room table I had decorated. He sat the tray over my lap. I couldn't deny I was starving. He left out the room and came back with another tray for himself. He got on the other side of the bed with his tray. I held my breath as he dug in the lasagna.

Dear, Vanity 2: Echon's Return   Nona Day

"You cook this?" He asked after two spoonful. I nervously nodded my head.

"It's good," he said nodding his head.

I smiled. "Really?"

"Yea, just lighten up on the garlic," he said.

"Thanks, Van walked me through it," I admitted.

"I like yo honesty. Most women pretend they can cook. At least you keep it real," he said.

I shrugged my shoulders. "I don't want to disappoint my future husband whenever I do meet him. At least he will know what to expect with me. I mean I will take cooking classes if it'll make him happy, but I don't plan on being Betty Crocker." He laughed.

"The hotel bar was crazy tonight. Some kind of convention going on. I had to stay and help. I tried calling you. I started to worry when you didn't answer," he admitted.

I looked at my phone to see the numerous missed calls from him. "I fell asleep. Sorry, for overreacting." He nodded his head.

"You have an MBA. Why are you working at a restaurant and bar?" I asked.

Dear, Vanity 2: Echon's Return   Nona Day

"It works for me," he simply said. I didn't understand what that meant but I didn't understand anything about him. I guess his main source of income was trafficking drugs. Why did I have to go and fall for the worst kind of guy? They were fun in my college years, but not to build a life with.

We enjoyed dinner getting to know each other on a more personal level. He told me his father left when he was thirteen. He has a rocky relationship with his mother. I still felt like it was something he wasn't telling me. Of course, I asked was he married or committed to anyone. He assured me he wasn't. After we were done eating, he took the trays back downstairs and cleaned up the kitchen. I had fallen asleep from drinking the bottle of wine. I felt his arm wrap around my waist and pull me closer to his naked body spooning me.

"I don't want to play this crazy game with you anymore. I really like you," I admitted in a whisper.

"I like you too, Zelly," he murmured in my ear. As much as I wanted to feel him inside me, I didn't want to end this night on our sexual chemistry. I already know that it was off the radar. I wanted to feel our mental connection.

I guess he was exhausted from work. He started snoring like a bear. I was going to be cranky in the morning from lack of sleep, but I wasn't going to complain. Laying next to him is worth it.

Vanity

Echon was overwhelmed with emotion when we went to the lounge. He loved everything I had done with the place. Being the man that stole my heart, he surprised me with a birthday cake with candles for each year he missed. It was a reminder of our first date. We took a stroll through the neighborhood and he gave me the most precious gift. We walked through the alley that led to his old apartment. I thought he was getting ready to break into his old apartment until he pulled the key out. He had furnished the apartment the way I remembered it. Come to find out, he purchased the entire building. We stayed the night making love to each other.

When I finished shopping with Zelda, I went home to my men, but they weren't home. I decided to visit Emmanuel. I walked into a waiting room full of chaos. The family was arguing amongst each other. Emmanuel's mother was in a corner praying and crying with all the commotion going on. I didn't want any parts of the argument, so I made my way to Emmanuel's room. There was still no improvement on his condition. I sat beside him and said my daily prayer I had with him. I applied lip balm to his dry lips and talked to him like he could hear every word I said. His mother walked in the room placing her hand on my shoulder.

"I didn't know you was here," she said sitting in the empty seat next to his bed.

"There was a lot going on in the waiting room, so I came straight to his room. How are you doing?" I asked. She looked tired and stressed.

"I'm fine, chile. Just tired from all the bickering back and forth with them damn fools," she said shaking her head.

"What's going on?" I asked curiously.

"Half doesn't have the faith to believe he can pull through this. The other half is saying they want to take him off the ventilator for his insurance and assets," she said.

Emmanuel was a wealthy man. He invested his money. He wasn't a millionaire, but he was wealthy. He was one of the investors in the project me and Quran started rebuilding the community.

"Don't let them take him off until you are at peace with it. Ultimately it's your decision," I told her.

She looked at me. "He loved you enough to let you go." I didn't understand her statement.

She placed her hand over mine. "He told me about EJ's father's return. He always knew he would struggle with having a place in your heart. He accepted having a place in your life. With the love of your life returning, there was no place for Emmanuel. He made peace with that."

Tears started to fall from my eyes. "How do you know this?"

"He came to talk to me after returning from New Orleans. He felt it in his soul that it was over between you and him. You are a good woman Vanity. My son knows that. You have an aurora about you that makes it hard not to love you. I wanted to be angry with you, but I couldn't. I know you never would hurt Em intentionally. Stop with the tears of guilt. You deserve this happiness God has granted you. I see the light in your eyes. I truly believe God gifts us with one great love. You have yours back in your life. Don't let guilt and doubt ruin it. When Emmanuel wakes up, he'll find that kind of love." She pulled me into her arms and comforted me as I sobbed softly. We sat and talked with Emmanuel until his father came in.

SOUL Publications

Dear, Vanity 2: Echon's Return   Nona Day

*****

When I got home, my heart was filled with so much peace and love. I walked out the back door to see my two men throwing the football. EJ waved at me while Echon smiled. I went to the bedroom and dressed comfortable to prepare dinner. A couple of hours later, I was sitting at the dinner table enjoying my family. I listened as EJ told Echon about the Fortnite game he can't get enough of playing. It was time to tell him about us being a family. I cleared my throat to get Echon's attention. He nodded his head.

"EJ, we want to talk to you about things since your father has returned. I know all of this is overwhelming for you," I said.

"Mama, I'm only a kid. I don't know what that word means," he said.

Echon chuckled. "What she really trying to say is we love you and want you to be okay with us being a family."

EJ shrugged his shoulders. "Okay. I'm cool with that."

"EJ do you understand what that means?" I asked.

"Yes ma'am. It means you and Daddy will be doing all that mushy stuff around me like Uncle Tree and Aunt Nika be doing," he said turning up his face. We laughed. Our child was growing up way too fast.

"Is Mr. Em going to be mad?" He asked glancing at us.

"No. He wants us to be happy. He knows being with Echon makes us happy," I told him.

He looked at Echon. "So Daddy, you gone get Mama pregnant and give me a lil brother I can beat up?"

Echon almost choked on the water he had in his mouth. "Where you learn this stuff from?"

"Khalil," he said smiling.

"I gotta have a talk with this Khalil," Echon said directing his statement to me. I nodded my head in agreement.

"Mama can we give Daddy all his gifts now?" EJ asked excited. Echon gave me a strange look.

"Yea, we sure can," I said standing up. I told Echon to stay seated until we came back. Me and EJ retrieved the box of gifts.

Dear, Vanity 2: Echon's Return   Nona Day

I sat the box on the dinner table. "Every year we remembered you on your birthday by buying you a gift. EJ made you a birthday card every year. I know it's not your birthday, but happy birthday."

"Happy Birthday Daddy," EJ said happily. Echon sat there with his head down. I knew he didn't want to show how emotional he was, so I told EJ to come in the den with me to give Daddy some time alone.

A while later, Echon walked in the den with all the birthday cards in his hand. He kneeled down to be eye level with EJ. "Out of all the gifts in the box, these cards mean the most to me."

They gave each other a father and son hug that melted my heart. He walked over and sat next to me giving me a soft kiss.

"See, that's the stuff that makes my stomach hurt," EJ said holding his stomach. I giggled.

"Go setup the game. I'll be there in a few," Echon said to him. He ran out of the den. I yelled for him to stop running in the house.

Dear, Vanity 2: Echon's Return   Nona Day

"There's another gift for you in the spare bedroom. It was too big to carry," I said. I took him by the hand to lead him to the spare bedroom.

"I was wondering why this door was locked," he said as I unlocked the door. When we stepped inside, he walked over admiring the vintage record player.

"I found it on eBay. I was in a bidding war with one other person, but I wasn't going to let it get away. I never imagined you would be standing here looking at it. I just wanted to have it to play your records that I've grown to love," I said.

He walked over to me. His face was so serious. "We gotta buy a bigger house Vanity."

"Why?" I asked with worry.

"Things I want to do to you isn't appropriate for a child's ears. You know how you scream," he said smiling. I giggled and tapped him in the chest.

"Since you know who you are, when is your birthday?" I asked.

"May 24th, but until he gets old enough to understand, we'll continue with the birthday he knows," he replied.

Dear, Vanity 2: Echon's Return   Nona Day

Echon went into EJ's bedroom to play the game with him while I cleaned the kitchen. I was in the bed studying some medical books when he came in the bedroom. He took a shower and got into bed. He had a familiar look on his face.

"When are you leaving?" I asked.

He stared at me. "Tomorrow afternoon. I'm coming back Vanity."

"I know," I said. I was scared, but I didn't want to admit it. I needed him to be focused on whatever he needed to do. I've accepted whatever it takes to build a life with him and EJ.

Echon

Tree picked me up from the airport in Colombia. We wasted no time driving to Putumayo. It was a part of Colombia where the majority of cocoa leaves are grown. Tree and Yella Boy went to North Carolina to search the house for any information that would lead me to my cousin or Shavonna, one of my uncle's wives. With just a phone number, Genius was able to track Shavonna in Colombia. Dose sent a soldier on his team to trail her. She led him to the cocoa fields that they took from Bull. He reported the fields were surrounded by a militia of soldiers. I remembered everything Chiraq told me. They would only obey orders from my cousin or Shavonna. I needed to get close to Shavonna. She could either get them to stand down or die. I wanted to avoid a war full of killing. We followed Shavonna from her hotel to Bull's jungle that was taken from him. A hidden gate covered by bushes opened and her car drove through.

"Now, how da fuck we getting in there?" Tree asked.

Dear, Vanity 2: Echon's Return   Nona Day

"We ain't going nowhere. I am. I need for you to go back home. If I'm not back in a week, give this to Vanity," he said.

"What da fuck? Come on man. Don't do this shit to her again. Don't do this to us. You got a fuckin' army willing to go to war with you," he pleaded.

"You know I'm a one man army. I would never take soldiers into a war with me. Trust me, I got this. I'll see you back in Nola," I said jumping out the car and slipping inside the jungle.

By the time I had made it to the house in the jungle, mosquitos and bugs had eaten me alive. I don't know what bit me, but I felt like I was getting sick. I was pouring in sweat, but felt cold. It was easy hiding because everyone was busy working. The soldiers kept their eyes on the workers. Rage consumed me as I looked at the small children working in the fields. Men were groping women and shouting obscenities to them as they worked. The male workers kept their heads down. I understood their situation. If they spoke up, they would be killed. I watched in the bushes as Shavonna walked out the house. She walked up to the three men that were sexually violating the women.

Dear, Vanity 2: Echon's Return   Nona Day

Without hesitation, she put two bullets in each of their heads.

"Let them be an example! They are here to work, not fulfill your sick, disgusting and perverted dreams. Now, burn the damn bodies," she said before walking inside the house.

The men tending to the dead bodies gave me the opportunity to slip inside the house. I felt like I was going to faint. I started vomiting. I emptied my stomach and slipped through the back door. I was relieved to see Shavonna was in the house alone. She paced the floor with her phone to her ear. She screamed angrily over the phone to Thomas. She demanded to know when he was coming to Colombia. She was tired of babysitting the militia. She ranted about having her freedom. I waited until her call ended. I stepped into her eyesight. She gasped for breath and dropped her phone. I opened my mouth to say something, but nothing came out. I collapsed on the floor.

I awakened with a dry mouth, feeling like I had been hit by a semi-truck. I didn't have the fever anymore. Even though I was sluggish, I felt better than I did before I passed out. I slowly started sitting up in the bed. I stopped when I heard a gun cock. I looked across the room to see Shavonna standing nervously staring at me. She was so rattled the gun was shaking in her hand.

"You are supposed to be dead," she said.

"Is that what Thomas told you? What makes you think I'm supposed to be dead?" I asked.

"He said they killed you," she said. I had no clue who they were.

"Put the gun down Shavonna. You have an army outside. I can't harm you," I assured her. She slowly lowered the gun.

"He said Bull's team killed you after you failed at killing Bull," she said.

"I never shot Bull. Thomas barged in the room and failed at killing him. I've been looking for his bitch ass ever since. Where is he?" I asked standing up.

"I don't know. He sent us here to take over the fields. We did as he said because he was the one in charge now. Bull's men killed Kasim," she said.

"No the fuck they didn't. Thomas killed his own father. Don't act like you wasn't in on it," I said.

"I swear I wasn't. I loved Kasim, but I was done with his lifestyle. I wanted out. I wanted to live my own life. Kasim wasn't there when Thomas returned. He told me you were killed by Bull's men. I only did what he said because he said it was Kasim's orders. That's why we took over the jungle. Thomas called me later and told me he was also killed by Bull's men. He said it was unsafe for me to return because they were seeking revenge on everyone with a connection to Kasim," she ranted.

"You control the army?" I asked.

"Yes, but I promise Atsu I had nothing to do with whatever Thomas has going on. Kasim never wanted things to go down like this. He just wanted you to have what was rightfully yours. Kasim could've been sought revenge for your parents' death, but he didn't. He felt like that right belonged to you and your brother. When you walked in here, I was on the phone with Thomas, because I wanted out of all of this. This isn't what Kasim wanted. He's turned the army into a bunch of gorillas. The only reason I stay is to protect those workers. I can only do so much."

It was something in her eyes that made me believe her. I needed her to convince them to take me as their leader. If she wanted her life and freedom she would agree.

"Are those workers here voluntarily?" I asked.

"Some are. I come daily to make sure they are being treated fairly. I let the ones leave that want to leave. Some are too afraid to speak up though," she said.

"You want your life and freedom?" I asked. She nodded her head.

I gave her instructions on what to do. I followed her outside to the fields. She gathered all the soldiers and workers. I listened as she told them she was no longer in charge. She told them who I was and about my father's legacy. All the soldiers raised a fist and bowed their heads to me. She stepped back and let me take over. I asked all the workers that didn't want to be here to raise their hands. A few women raised their hands. I demanded those women and all the kids be released. I would have no parts of child labor. Any workers that chose to work would have a set time to work and be paid generously for their hard labor. I gave soldiers instructions on how I wanted the workers to be treated. A few soldiers loaded up a bus to return the ones that chose to leave to their homes while everyone else went back to work.

I turned to face Shavonna. "Who tried to kill Emmanuel."

She gave me a puzzled look. "Who is that?"

"He was shot in his car in Atlanta multiple times," I said. She still had a bewildered look on her face. It was obvious she had no clue what I was talking about.

"Give me the phone number you use to call Thomas," I said.

She gave me her phone. "You can read all the messages I sent him if you don't believe me. He calls and texts me from three different numbers." I didn't have to check her phone. I know she was telling the truth.

"Are you financially stable?" I asked.

"Kasim always made sure I would be well taken care of if he wasn't here," she said. I nodded my head.

"Pick a soldier to make sure things stay in order until I return," I said. She yelled out the name Baron. He walked over looking like one big ass muscle with a murderous look on his face. I gave him instructions on what to do until I return. He bowed his head.

"Stop doing that shit. I'm yo fuckin' equal. I'm not a god," I said. He stared me in the eyes. A big goofy ass grin spread across his face.

"Gotcha Chief," he said. I chuckled and shook my head.

"He's a teddy bear but don't let that fool you. That fool is a vicious savage," she said smiling. It was no doubt he was.

"You can go," I said.

"Are you serious?" She asked.

"Yea," I said. She dropped to her knees to kiss my feet.

"You kiss my damn feet, I'll kill yo ass," I said staring down at her. She slowly stood up and thanked me.

"Come on, you my ride back to the city. What the fuck bit me anyway?" I asked.

"A scorpion. One of the women workers keeps a remedy because workers get bit frequently," she said.

Two Days Later

Dear, Vanity 2: Echon's Return   Nona Day

It took Genius no time to track down Thomas. He was laid up in a hotel in Las Vegas. I found him at a casino gambling away thousands of dollars that he killed for. Dose had called up some connections he had here for me to do what I needed to do. I watched him from afar until he finally decided to give up. I watched him leave the hotel casino. He had a room in the hotel. The hotel belonged to a former street king named King, so it wasn't hard getting the key to the room. When we got inside the room he was in the shower. Max slipped inside and covered his head with a plastic bag. He kept the bag over his head until he almost stopped breathing. He laughed the entire time he watched Thomas struggle to breathe. I didn't know Max personally, but I've heard stories about his enjoyment of torturing his hits. When Thomas finally stopped coughing from trying to catch his breath, he looked at me.

"Hey cousin," I said gazing down at him.

"It was father! He made me do everything!" He lied knowing his life was in jeopardy.

"Get up and get dressed," I said.

"Please! You can have everything. Just let me live," he pleaded.

Dear, Vanity 2: Echon's Return   Nona Day

"Didn't the man tell you to get yo punk ass up? Now move!" Max barked kicking him in the side. He yelped from the pain as he slowly got up.

"So, you gone let me help? I heard you do great work," Max asked smiling at me. I ignored his question. If it came to torturing, he can have it. I don't think it would come to that. Thomas wasn't strong enough to hold out. I could probably get what I needed from him right here in the hotel, but his life ends tonight. I couldn't do it here.

*****

We took him to one of Max's warehouses where he does his work. Max was rapping some shit I don't know as he tied Thomas down to a table. He was stretched out with his arms and legs tied down. He pleaded and cried for mercy. I had none to give. I asked him several questions and he didn't hesitate to give me the answers. Max was mad because he was making it too easy.

"What kind of bitch nigga you is? You supposed to withhold the information as long as possible. You pissing me da fuck off. I haven't showed my artwork in years. My wife be tripping and shit. She don't like me torturing and killing people. I tried to explain to her I only do it to bad people," Max ranted in frustration.

He looked at me. "You ever loved a bitch so much, you want to kill just thinking about another nigga being with her?" I wanted to laugh at his crazy ass, but I knew how he felt about that type of love. That question might've just saved a life.

I had all the information I needed. He was the one that shot me. He knew I was alive for years. As long as my uncle didn't know of my whereabouts, he didn't feel threatened. Things changed when he tried to kill me. His plan was to kill me and my brother. He wanted the legacy that he felt belonged to him. He felt like his father neglected him and gave my brother all his love and attention. I don't care about his reasoning. He had to die.

"I have all the information I need," I said looking at Max.

"What now? You killing him or letting him go?" Max asked anxiously.

"Do whatever you want," I told him. I needed to make one more stop before going home to my family.

"I'm gone record my work and send it to you. Take my car. I'll pick it up from the airport," Max said starting a chainsaw. I shook my head and left.

*****

Atlanta, Ga

I was beyond exhausted from all the traveling, but I was determined to do what needs to be done before returning to her. I knocked on the door. Quran opened the door and welcomed me inside. I declined a drink and we sat in his den just chatting like two normal dudes. I was still contemplating how to handle this delicate situation. Thoughts of Vanity and EJ was the only reason he was still living.

"How long did you know I was alive?" I asked pulling my Nine out. His eyes grew big. He quickly glanced over at his gun that lay on an end table.

"You'll be dead before you touch it," I warned him.

He took a deep breath. "It's obvious you already know everything."

After my uncle brought me to my father's house, Thomas went seeking all the information he could on me. It took him to Atlanta and Quran. He didn't want me back, because of his love for Vanity and he felt I was coming back to take what he built with Vanity. I had no intentions of ever interfering with the work him and Vanity has done. It's something I wanted to happen, but I can't take credit for their hard work. Emmanuel walked in the bar and overheard his conversation with Thomas. Emmanuel threatened to tell Vanity about him working with Thomas to take over everything. Thomas thought Bull's team would kill me after he tried to kill Bull. He didn't understand the value of love and loyalty. Quran was going to let everything happen because he knew it would get me out of the way. He orchestrated the failed attempt on Emmanuel's life.

"You came back here like shit was the same. Mothafucka I raised yo son. I was her backbone when she felt like dying. We built that community up. I wasn't going to let you come back and take what I built," he said.

"I never wanted what you built. I came back for what always belonged to me. That's my family. You should be dead right now. The only reason you still living is because of Vanity and EJ. She's suffered too much loss in her life. I don't want to see her hurt anymore. EJ looks up to you like a father. I would never take for granted what

Dear, Vanity 2: Echon's Return   Nona Day

you did for them, but you are dead to me. I don't know how, but you better find a way to dismiss yourself from their lives without it hurting them," I said.

"I have enough shit on you to send you to prison for life," he threatened me.

I chuckled. "I knew that was coming. I have just as much shit on you. I always have your mother, grandparents, and your sibling's address. Before I let you take me away from them, I will make you sit and watch me torture them slowly until they take their last breath. I understand why you did what you did now. That kind of love that will make you kill is beautiful and dangerous."

I stood up. "I expect you to show your face one more time before you disappear. You have one week to do what you need to do."

The moment I went to open the door, I heard him cock his gun. I turned around to face him. "You can't have my life. Sorry brother."

One shot to my chest sent me flying against the door. The sting from the bullet was painful, but I was able to aim at him. Both of us let off a couple of shots.

One Week Later

Zelda

The past week I've felt like I've been floating on a natural high. I've been spending my evenings after work with Jedrek. It hasn't been all about sex. We've been spending time getting to know each other. I don't know what this man has done to me. He has me acting like a love sick teenager. I've done something I know I shouldn't have done. Every time I think about it, I get sick to my stomach. I needed so desperately to vent to Vanity, but she is dealing with too much right now. Echon hasn't returned yet, and she's going crazy. We flew to New Orleans for Baby Glady's birthday party. Me and Vanity stayed at a luxury hotel. Of course, EJ wanted to stay with Tree and Nika.

"Vanity stop stressing. He's coming back," I said flopping down next to her on the couch.

"I know he's okay. I feel it inside me. I just want him to hurry home," she said smiling.

"Good, because I have a situation. You are going to be so disappointed in me. I don't know what I was thinking," I said worriedly. She sat up giving me her full attention.

Dear, Vanity 2: Echon's Return   Nona Day

I dropped my head and spoke in a low voice. "I'm pregnant."

The room was silent for a few seconds until she jumped up and started screaming with joy. I've never been on any type of birth control. I've always used condoms. I did get pregnant in college, because the condom broke. Having the abortion was the hardest thing I had done. Vanity was my strength that pulled me out of depression. Even though she was deep in her religion at the time, she never judged me. That morning I had sex with Jedrek on the beach was when I got pregnant. I was so caught up in the moment I didn't want to stop. I felt so connected to him. When reality set in that I had unprotected sex, I should've gotten the morning after pill. I didn't want to take the pill. Something inside wouldn't let me do it.

"Vanity calm down. This isn't a good thing," I told her.

"Yes, it is. I'm going to be Aunt V!" She said dancing. I couldn't help but laugh. She has no rhythm. She danced with excitement until she was exhausted.

"I think I did it intentionally," I said shamefully.

Dear, Vanity 2: Echon's Return   Nona Day

"What?" She asked.

"You know I've always been careful about getting pregnant since the abortion. He warned me he was getting ready to come. He tried lifting me off of him, but I wouldn't move. I bought a morning after pill soon as we got back to New Orleans. I didn't take it Van," I said.

"Is he mad?" She asked.

"I haven't told him. We've been getting along so well. I've fallen in love with him. What if this runs him away?"

"You won't know until you tell him Zee. If he doesn't want to be the daddy, I'll be the daddy," she said smiling. I giggled.

"He's coming here tonight. I'll tell him then. Just be ready to comfort me if he breaks my heart," I said.

"As much as I've cried on your shoulder, you know I've got you," she said smiling.

"I thought you would be disappointed in me," I said.

She laughed. "Zee I could never be disappointed in you. Besides I was so in lust and love, I never considered birth control. Hell, I never thought of diseases. Damn, what was I thinking?"

"About getting your cherry plucked," I said smiling.

"And I'm so thankful I had EJ. I can't imagine my life without him," she said getting emotional.

"Okay, no tears. I'm hungry. Let's go over to Nika's for this barbecue," I said standing up.

She sat there smiling at her phone. I knew it had to be Echon. She looked up at me with the brightest eyes.

"He said he'll be home soon. He said he hopes I'm ready to be his wife," she said as a tear slid down her cheek. Damn hormones caused tears to slide down my cheeks.

Later

We were all enjoying Baby Glady's birthday in the backyard. I loved the bond everyone had with each other. It started to make me miss my parents. I was blessed to be born with loving parents. I worried what they would think about me being pregnant with no husband. Hell, I don't even know if I could call Jedrek my boyfriend.

"There goes your boyfriend," Zuri said nodding toward the patio door. I looked over my shoulder to see him standing there in all his delicious dark chocolate. He just

Dear, Vanity 2: Echon's Return   Nona Day

stood there staring down at me. I wanted to run over, hug him with a deep, wet kiss but I wasn't comfortable with pubic affection. He walked over to where the guys were standing around the grill.

"He acts just like Yella Boy, weird as hell," Nika said. We all laughed.

"I think they are both adorable," Worth said. It was good seeing her smiling again. Bull was doing much better. He checked himself out of the hospital a couple of days ago. She wasn't too pleased with that, but she knows how stubborn he is. She won the battle today making him stay home and rest.

The rest of the day was great until it was time to go. I was going to use the bathroom when I walked up on an intense conversation between Jedrek and Yella Boy. There was fire in both of their eyes. I looked at them.

"What da fuck you want?" Jedrek asked angrily.

"Nothing with yo bitch ass!" I shouted before storming back out on the deck.

There is no way I'm having a baby by this fool. I'm getting an abortion soon as I get back to Atlanta. I just

Dear, Vanity 2: Echon's Return   Nona Day

won't tell Vanity about it. I know she'll convince me to have it. No need to tell him. It's obvious he doesn't give a fuck. He left the house after the altercation with Yella Boy. I thought he would show up at my room later that night, but he never did.

Vanity

"Come on! Get up! We have some pampering to do!" Zelda yelled as she just jumped up and down on my bed.

I threw a pillow at her. "Get off my bed. It's too early. Stop jumping! You are disturbing my niece inside you."

She laughed and flopped down on the bed. "Come on, I need to go pamper myself. I'm feeling bloated and ugly. I've booked us a day at a spa with full treatment. And makeovers and pedicures. If that nigga don't know what he has in me. I'll just love myself."

I smiled at her. "That's my Z-Dawg."

She laughed hysterically. "You are so damn corny sometimes."

I pulled myself out of bed and got dressed. We spent the entire day pampering ourselves. I was in a great mood because I knew he would be home soon. I decided to style my hair with some long, black, body waved Peruvian extensions. The day was therapeutic. All I needed now was for Echon to come home. I thought he would answer his phone, since he texted me yesterday. I wasn't answering any of my calls or texts. I tried pushing the worry out of my mind. I told myself he would be home soon.

"Where we going now, since we all pampered and dolled up?" I asked as she drove.

"Worth's house for wine. Stop calling that's man's phone. He'll be home," she said smiling.

"He's not replying to my texts," I said.

"You worry too much," she said.

*****

I was surprised to see everyone at the house. I thought it was just going to be all the ladies, but all the men were here also. When we got to the front door, Zelda just walked the house.

"Zee, we can't just walk in here," I said standing at the door.

"Worth said to just come in. Everyone is in the back of the house. They'll never hear us," she said dragging me inside. I reluctantly followed her through the enormous house until we reached the back double door.

Dear, Vanity 2: Echon's Return   Nona Day

She looked back at me with a big silly grin. "You ready?"

"I just hope Bull doesn't kill us for just walking in his house," I said nervously.

"I can't stand this. I'm so excited. You deserve every bit of this Van," she said getting emotional.

"What are you talking about?" I asked.

When she opened the door, my mouth dropped. It was the most beautiful scene I had ever seen. Their entire humongous backyard was decorated like a fairytale. The colors were white and light blue. It was the picture image of heaven that I held in my heart. There were holograms of clouds with beautiful chocolate angels playing harps. The entire ground was covered with clouds. Chairs were lined up side by side with an aisle between them. The aisle led to a pearly, beautiful gate. On the other side of the gate was a rainbow with all my favorite colors.

"What is this?" I asked Zelda.

"It's your wedding day. He's waiting for you. We have to get dressed. Please don't cry. You are going to ruin your makeup," she said with her eyes full of tears. I fanned my face trying to dry the tears before they fell.

Dear, Vanity 2: Echon's Return   Nona Day

I followed her upstairs where I slipped on the most, beautiful fairytale dress. I always told Zelda what kind of wedding and dress I wanted to be married in. I stood in the mirror admiring myself. She pleaded with me not to cry, but I couldn't help it. My dream was coming true. She dapped the tears as they from my face. When I thanked her with a hug, both of us couldn't stop the tears.

"I told you y'all was going to cry. Let me touch y'all up," Love said walking in the room.

She quickly fixed my makeup. They left me in the room by myself for a few minutes. I thanked God for blessing me with so much in my life. I may not have the family I was born into, but he blessed me with a family that was just as loving. I made my way downstairs. I realized I didn't have anyone to walk me down the aisle. When the doors opened my new favorite R&B singer, Rush was singing his new love ballad. His voice sent chills through me every time I listened to him. I turned my head to see Dose approaching me with a beautiful, white horse dressed like a unicorn. *Live your life like you see unicorns and rainbows every day.* Dose helped me on the horse. I had to ride it sideways because of my dress. He walked beside the horse as it carried me down the aisle. My heart fluttered when I spotted Echon dressed like a Prince in his white tuxedo. Tree stood beside him as his best man. EJ stood beside him as the ring bearer. Zelda stood on my side in her beautiful maid of honor dress. Baby Gladys was my flower girl.

When the horse stopped, I didn't wait for Dose to help me off. Everyone laughed when I hopped off the horse and rushed over to Echon throwing my arms around him. He grimaced like he was in pain. I stepped back and examined him from head to toe.

"I'm okay. I'll explain later," he said smiling at me.

"I love you so much," I said gazing up into his eyes.

He placed his hand on the side of my face. "I promise to make your life feel like heaven on earth if you'll be my wife."

"Yes. I will be yours forever," I said as tears started to fall. He opened the gate and we stood under the rainbow where we exchanged vows.

The pastor introduced us as Mr. & Mrs. Echon. We gave each other a deep passionate kiss as everyone applauded and screamed with joy.

I leaned over and whispered in his ear. "What is our last name now? We have to change EJ's name."

"It's Bello. I've already changed his last name. I'm still Echon. We will only use my last name for legal purposes," he said.

There was no use in my asking how he changed his name. With this family, anything is possible. I simply nodded my head. It was only right we share our first dance together with Al Green's *Love and Happiness.* We ended the evening dancing and laughing until our hearts were content.

*****

I couldn't wait to get inside the hotel room. I started ripping his clothes off on the elevator. The beautiful dress was ruined by the time he tore it off of me. It had too many snaps for him to take the time to unbutton. He ripped my bra and panties off. I was bent over the kitchen isle in my heels with him deep inside me. My butt cheeks clapped against his pelvis as he rammed inside me. His rock hard rod was throwing and growing inside me. I couldn't stop coming. My essence was gushing like a waterfall.

Dear, Vanity 2: Echon's Return   Nona Day

"Oooh Gggggod! Right there! I'm about to come again!" I screamed as my body quivered. He plunged deeper inside me causing my knees to buckle as I exploded. He pulled out of me and sat me on the counter spreading my legs as wide as they would go. He took my heels off and sucked each one of my toes into his mouth before licking his way up to my thighs. His tongue lapped over my dripping mound. I arched my back off the counter pleading for more of him. His tongue became a ferocious tornado lapping circles around my clit, sucking up the rain that poured from me. I screamed out his name with love and passion as my soul floated in a cosmic galaxy.

He lifted me off the counter and thrust himself inside me again. He gave me more than I could handle against the kitchen wall all the to the bedroom. His deep, sexy voice made me come harder as he poured his heart and soul out to me in my ear while drilling inside me.

"I can't fuckin' stop! You feel so damn good!" He barked pinning my legs over his shoulders.

He buried his face in the crook of my neck and put a hump in his back. He started annihilating my drenched tunnel. He growled and grunted as he hammered inside me.

Dear, Vanity 2: Echon's Return   Nona Day

I clawed and scratched his back and butt as I tried to take everything, he was giving me.

"I love you so got damn much!" He murmured in my ear.

He was insatiable. He pulled out and licked his way down between my legs making sure to stop and give my breasts his full attention. He lifted my butt in the air and stroked his tongue back and forth. He moaned and groaned like I was the most delicious treat on earth. He laid on his back pulling me on top of him. He slammed me down on him. I gave him all that I had left in me. I twirled my hips and bounced on his throbbing penis. I squeezed my walls around his shaft as I rocked back and forth.

"Fuck! Keep doing that! I'm 'bout to come!" He roared as he licked and sucked on my breasts.

"Eeeeechon! Sssshhhhit! I'm coooomming!" I screamed. My essence gushed from me.

"Aaaarrrghh! Don't got damn stop! Keep going!" He demanded with a scowl on his face. Gushy, splashing, wet sounds echoed along with our cries of ecstasy. I

Dear, Vanity 2: Echon's Return   Nona Day

pressed the palms of my hands in his chest and continued bringing him to his breaking point.

"Aaaarrrggghhh! Ggggrrrrrrr!" He roared like a barbaric animal exploding deep inside me.

He sat up and flipped me over on my back. He started pounding inside me like our lives depended on it. My hands dug into the coils on his head as he rammed inside me. I felt him getting ready to come again. I pleaded to taste him. He pulled out and I wrapped my lips around his shaft tasting a mixture of our love. His body shook violently as I drained him of his soul and love.

Epilogue

Two Months Later

I never wore vests. I was thankful I listened to Tree this time. I had more than my own life to consider. That vest saved my life. Vanity finally let me buy the bigger house we needed. I had a seven bedroom, ten bathroom house built with a in ground swimming pool, enormous backyard and a man cave for me and EJ. It was hard telling her about Quran. I didn't want to kill him. I still had love for him. I didn't like his actions, but I understood the lengths a man would go to for the woman he loves. She took his death better than I expected she would. EJ took it hard. That was the first time he ever truly experienced losing someone close to him. Vanity understood my actions. It was no surprise to me or Vanity when she got pregnant on our wedding night. When we returned from our honeymoon, she went to visit Emmanuel daily. She had faith he would pull through and he did. He gave us his blessing and wished us well. Zelda moved into our old house since it is closer to us. There's a lot of whispering between her and Vanity. Vanity seems to be frustrated with Zelda sometimes. I don't get involved in their friendship. I know whatever it is, they will work through it. As far as my father's legacy, Bull made me an offer to run everything as his equal partner. I don't care about any of it, but for my father's namesake I accepted his offer. I thought Vanity would be upset, but she said she understood and wouldn't expect any less from me. Our love for each other has only grown stronger. I don't know if there is a heaven, but I thanked God daily for giving me a chance to experience heaven on earth.

The End

For updates, sneak peeks and future releases: Nona Day on Facebook

SOUL Publications